Life After Debt

Third Edition

Free Yourself From the Burden of
Money Worries Once and for All

By
Bob Hammond

Copyright © 2000 by Bob Hammond

All rights reserved under the Pan-American and International Copyright Conventions. This book may not be reproduced, in whole or in part, in any form or by any means electronic or mechanical, including photocopying, recording, or by any information storage and retrieval system now known or hereafter invented, without written permission from the publisher, The Career Press.

Life After Debt

Cover design by Barry Littmann

Printed in the U.S.A. by Book-mart Press

To order this title, please call toll-free 1-800-CAREER-1 (NJ and Canada: 201-848-0310) to order using VISA or Master Card, or for further information on books from Career Press.

The Career Press, Inc., 3 Tice Road, PO Box 687, Franklin Lakes, NJ 07417

Library of Congress Cataloging-in-Publication Data

Hammond, Bob.

Life after debt : free yourself from the burden of money worries once and for all / by Bob Hammond.—3rd ed.

p. cm.

Includes index.

ISBN 1-56414-421-6 (pbk.)

1. Consumer credit—United States. 2. Debtor and creditor—United States.

I. Title.

HG3756.U54 H365 1999

332.7'43—dc21 99-059730

Dedication

To Me-an.

Acknowledgments

Thanks to:

- ❑ Ron Fry, Stacey Farkas, Jodi Brandon, Jackie Michaels, and all of the staff at Career Press for making this third edition the best ever.
- ❑ Peder Lund, Jon Ford, and the gang at Paladin Press for a great job on helping me put together the original version of *Life After Debt*.
- ❑ Ethan Ellenberg for putting the deal together.
- ❑ Bob and Larry at Newman Communications for a great promotional campaign.
- ❑ Ron Vervick and Michael Soccio for helping me keep my head pointed in the right direction.
- ❑ My attorney, Winfield Payne III, who provided me with much-needed legal advice and assistance.
- ❑ Mom and Dad for your unconditional love and support.
- ❑ My son, Robert, for being my inspiration and hope.
- ❑ Jen Reed for helping me overcome writer's block and get my priorities back in order.

Contents

Part 3: Appendices

Author's Note

There have been some alarming developments in the credit system since the last edition of *Life After Debt* was published in 1996 that directly affect consumers. Here are some of the highlights:

- ❑ A record number of bankruptcy filings have triggered calls for reform by retailers and credit card companies.
- ❑ Continued abuses by credit reporting agencies have led to numerous lawsuits against credit bureaus and a revision of the Fair Credit Reporting Act.
- ❑ Law enforcement officials have shut down hundreds of fraudulent credit repair companies, and new legislation has been introduced to protect consumers from their deceptive business practices.
- ❑ Finally, an even more disturbing trend: Identification theft has become one of the fastest-growing new crimes. As a result of modern technology, i.e., the Internet, much of your personal information is available to anybody with access to a personal computer. Imagine discovering that someone else has used your social security number, address, and account numbers to charge thousands of dollars' worth of cash advances, services, and merchandise using your hitherto good credit.

The purpose of this newly revised edition of *Life After Debt* is to help prepare you for life in the new millennium. You will learn how to get out of debt, restore your credit, and protect yourself from credit abuses—once and for all!

Introduction

Why read this guide?

A few interesting statistics about debt

- According to the Federal Reserve, credit card debt rose at a nearly record pace to $1.3 trillion in January 1999.
- In 1998, personal bankruptcies hit a record high of $1.4 million.
- During the 1990s, more than 50 million Americans suffered income interruptions, job layoffs, or reduced incomes.
- More than two million Americans have had their homes foreclosed.
- After necessities, nearly 90 percent of the money Americans earn goes toward debts.
- In the 1990s, the Federal Trade Commission received more complaints about credit reporting abuses than all other problems combined.
- Approximately 30 million Americans are in trouble with the Internal Revenue Service (IRS).
- According to an October 1999 study released by the Consumer Federation of America and Primerica, a

financial services company, the typical household's consumer debts total more than half its assets, and half of all U.S. households have less than $1,000 in ready assets.

- ❑ More than 40 percent of American families earning less than $35,000 felt they were more likely to accumulate $500,000 by winning a lottery than through regular savings in a retirement fund.
- ❑ The average family has $3,000 in consumer debt.
- ❑ Ten percent of all families have consumer debt of $20,000 or more.
- ❑ According to a study by Virginia Polytechnic Institute, 54 percent of the workforce worries about their debt, 53 percent are dissatisfied with their financial condition, 34 percent rate their financial stress from "high" to "extreme," and 33 percent believe their money worries hinder their job performance.

10 warning signs

If any of these conditions apply to you, it's time to take a closer look at your budget. If three or more apply, you are in financial difficulty and should seek assistance as soon as possible.

1. Using credit to buy things you used to be able to buy with cash.
2. Getting loans or extensions to pay your debts.
3. Paying only the minimum amount due on charge cards.
4. Receiving overdue notices from creditors.
5. Using savings to pay bills that you used to pay from checking.
6. Borrowing on life insurance with little chance of repayment.
7. Depending on overtime pay to make ends meet each month.

8. Using your checking account "overdraft" to pay regular bills.
9. Juggling rent or mortgage money to pay other debts.
10. Using credit card cash advances to help pay living expenses.

Until now, people with credit problems could only go to books that offered tedious budget plans or vague interpretations of federal consumer law. These books often assume the reader's ability to adhere to strict payment schedules or implement complex legal strategies. They fail, however, to address the real problem: Most of us are not lawyers or accountants.

Few of us are inclined to carry out technical legal maneuvers or sophisticated financial strategies. Even fewer people can afford the services of a good financial advisor. Sometimes people just aren't able to pay anything to anyone. Millions of Americans are living on the edge of financial disaster, surviving only on the hope of next week's paycheck.

Life After Debt is a primer, the first of its kind, that teaches people to play the credit game and win—regardless of where they start. It provides practical solutions for every kind of credit-related problem through case histories, sample letters, and easy-to-follow procedures.

The purpose of this book is to help you break the bondage of debt and start over. It will guide you from the ravaging tyranny of financial slavery to the light of freedom. You will come to know the insidious nature of the beast as you discover how its ensnaring web weaves its way into your life. You will learn to fight back against an unfair system—and win—for yourself and your family.

May the eyes of your understanding be enlightened.

Part 1

Is there really life after debt?

Chapter 1

Counting the cost of credit

Ron and Angela decided to celebrate their first anniversary together by purchasing a top-of-the-line stereo system. Still living on a shoestring, they wanted to be sure of getting top value for their money, so they spent weeks reading stereo magazines and catalogs, visiting showrooms, and getting advice from their friends. Finally, they settled on the components they wanted. Then they went to the dealer they had chosen and, after a couple of hours of bargaining, agreed on a total price that was considerably under the list prices displayed on the floor. They signed an installment contract offered by the store and raced home with their car full of stereo components, feeling like robbers who had made a daring getaway.

◆◆◆

What's wrong with this picture?

The total interest Ron and Angela were committed to paying far exceeded the total dollar amount they had saved by their careful bargaining. It had never occurred to either Ron or Angela that they could profit by putting as much effort into shopping for credit as they had into choosing their stereo components.

Credit issuers are smart. They know human nature and buying habits inside out. That's why they're getting richer while you're getting deeper into debt. They have joined forces with the advertising industry to convince you that you can have everything your heart desires right now—even things you didn't know you wanted.

Consumers are made to feel guilty for not using credit or for not having a credit card. Have you ever made a purchase and been asked, "Will that be on your account today?" What the clerk is really saying is, "You are worthy enough to have a credit card, aren't you?"

People are fooled into becoming debtors by thinking of debt as credit. Some people even get a certain amount of gratification from flashing a wallet full of plastic in front of others as if it were some type of status symbol. How many times have you engaged in this game of credit card one-upmanship to see who can display the most prestigious credit card?

For most people, debt (credit) represents a fair exchange for the lifestyle they enjoy. Others find it a consuming whirlpool that sucks their creative talents continuously. These people have become unemployed or have lost their economic base. For them, debt is no longer a slight inconvenience—it is a rapidly growing monster. They experience a special type of hell with every mail delivery containing bills and registered letters. The stories they have heard concerning bill collectors, repossessions, and foreclosures take on a frightening reality. These people assume a sense of desperation, which is instantly communicated to potential employers or sources of income. These people may as well have a neon sign on their foreheads flashing LOSER. This sets up a vicious cycle. Debts cause desperation, desperation turns off employers, and debts get bigger.

The cycle begins when you promise to pay in the future for something you receive in the present. It starts when you charge a meal on your credit card, pay for an appliance on the installment plan, or take out a loan to pay for a house, school, or vacation. With credit, you can enjoy your purchase while you're paying for it—or you can make a purchase when you're lacking ready cash. But there are strings attached. What is borrowed must be paid back. Before borrowing or opening a credit account, you should always figure out how much it will cost you and whether you can afford it.

Finance charges and annual percentage rates

Credit costs vary. By remembering two terms, you can compare credit prices from different sources. The law says there are two pieces of information that must be shown to you in writing *before* you sign a credit contract or use a credit card—the finance charge and the annual percentage rate (APR).

All creditors—banks, stores, car dealers, credit card companies, finance companies, etc.—must state the cost of their credit in terms of the finance charge and the APR. Federal law does not set interest rates or other credit charges. But it does require their disclosure so that you can compare credit costs.

The finance charge is the total dollar amount you pay to use credit. It includes interest fees, as well as service charges and some credit-related insurance premiums. For example, borrowing $100 for a year might cost you $10 in interest. If there was also a service charge of $1, the finance charge would be $11.

The annual percentage rate is the percentage cost (or relative cost) of credit on a yearly basis. This is your key to comparing costs, regardless of the amount of credit or how long you have to repay it.

Again, suppose you borrow $100 for one year and pay a finance charge of $10. If you can keep the entire $100 for the whole year and then pay back $110 at the end of the year, you are paying an APR of 10 percent. But, if you repay the $100 and finance charge (a total of $110) in twelve monthly installments, you don't really get to use $100 for the whole year. In fact, you get to use less and less of that $100 each month. In this case, the $10 charge for credit amounts to an APR of 18 percent.

Comparison

Even when you understand the terms a creditor is offering, it's easy to underestimate the difference in dollars various terms can make. Suppose you're buying a $15,000 car. You put $3,000 down and need to borrow $12,000. Compare the three credit arrangements shown in the chart below. How do these choices stack up? The answer depends partly on what you need.

The lowest-cost loan is available from Creditor A at an APR of 14 percent over three years. If you were looking for lower monthly payments, you could get them by paying the loan off over a longer period of time. However, you would have to pay more in total costs.

A loan from Creditor B—also at a 14 percent APR but for four years—will add about $976 to your finance charge. If that four-year loan was available only from Creditor C, the APR of 15 percent would add another $290 or so to your finance charges as compared with Creditor B.

Other factors—such as the size of the down payment—will also make a difference. Be sure to look at all the terms before you make your choice.

Creditor	APR	Length of loan	Monthly payment	Total finance	Total
A	14%	3 years	$410.13	$2,767.04	$14,764
B	14%	4 years	$327.92	$3,740.16	$15,740
C	15%	4 years	$333.97	$4,030.08	$16,030

Cost of open-end credit

Open-end credit includes bank and department store credit cards, gasoline company cards, home equity lines, and check overdraft accounts that let you write checks for more than your actual balance with the bank. Open-end credit can be used again and again, generally until you reach a certain prearranged borrowing limit. Truth-in-lending laws require that open-end creditors tell you the terms of the credit plan so that you can shop and compare the costs involved.

When you're shopping for an open-end plan, the APR you're quoted represents only the periodic rate that you will be charged, figured on a yearly basis. (For instance, a creditor that charges 1.5 percent interest each month would quote you an 18 percent APR.)

Annual membership fees, transaction charges, and points are listed separately; they are not included in the APR. (A point is a service charge equal to one percent of the loan amount. Five points on a $100,000 loan, for example, equals an additional $5,000 fee to be paid to the lender.) Keep this in mind and compare all the costs involved in the plans, rather than just the APR.

Creditors must tell you when the finance charges begin on your account, so you know how much time you have before a finance charge is added. Creditors may give you a 25-day grace period, for example, to pay your balance in full before adding a finance charge.

Creditors also must tell you the method they use to figure the balance on which you pay a finance charge; the interest rate they charge is applied to this balance to come up with the finance charge. Creditors use a number of different methods to arrive at the balance. Study them carefully; they can affect your finance charge significantly. Here are some of the most common methods.

- ❏ *Adjusted balance method.* Creditors take the amount you owed at the beginning of the billing cycle and subtract any payments you made during that cycle. Purchases are not counted.
- ❏ *Previous balance method.* Creditors simply use the amount owed at the beginning of the billing cycle to come up with the finance charge.
- ❏ *Average daily balance method.* Creditors add your balances for each day in the billing cycle and then divide that total by the number of days in the cycle. Payments made during the cycle are subtracted in arriving at the daily amounts, and, depending on the plan, new purchases may or may not be included.
- ❏ *Two-cycle average daily balance method.* Creditors use the average daily balances for two billing cycles to compute your finance charge. Again, payments will be taken into account in figuring the balances, but new purchases may or may not be included.

Be aware that the amount of the finance charge may vary considerably depending on the method used, even for the same pattern of purchases and payments.

If you receive a credit card offer or an application, the creditor must give you information about APR and other important terms of the plan at that time. Likewise, with a home-equity plan, information must be given to you with an application.

Truth-in-lending laws do not set the rates or tell the creditor how to calculate finance charges—they only require that the creditor tell you the method that it uses. You should ask for an explanation of terms you don't understand.

Billing errors

There's an easy and effective way to straighten out billing errors. The Fair Credit Billing Act requires creditors to correct errors promptly and without damage to your credit rating.

The law defines a billing error as any charge:

- ❑ For something you didn't buy or for a purchase made by someone not authorized to use your account.
- ❑ That is not properly identified on your bill or is for an amount different from the actual purchase price or that was entered on a date different from the purchase date.
- ❑ For something that you did not accept on delivery or that was not delivered according to agreement.

Billing errors also include:

- ❑ Mistakes in arithmetic.
- ❑ Failure to reflect a payment or other credit to your account.
- ❑ Failure to mail the statement to your current address, provided you notified the creditor of an address change at least 20 days before the end of the billing period.
- ❑ A questionable item, or one for which you need additional information.

If you think your bill is wrong or want more information about it, follow these steps:

1. Notify the creditor in writing within 60 days after the bill was mailed. Be sure to write to the address the creditor lists for billing inquiries and include the following information:

   A. Your name and account number.

   B. A description of the error and why you believe it is wrong.

   C. The date and amount of the suspected error or the item you want explained.

2. Pay all parts of the bill that are not in dispute. While waiting for an answer, you do not have to pay the amount in question (the "disputed amount") or any minimum payments or finance charges that apply to it. The creditor must acknowledge your letter within 30 days, unless the problem can be resolved within that time. Within two billing periods, but in no case longer than 90 days, either your account must be corrected or you must be told why the creditor believes the bill is correct.

   If the creditor made a mistake, you do not have to pay any finance charges on the disputed amount. Your account must be corrected, and you must be sent an explanation of any amount you still owe.

   If no error is found, the creditor must send you an explanation of the reasons for that determination and promptly send a statement of what you owe, which may include any finance charges that have accumulated and any minimum payments you missed while you were questioning the bill. You then have the time usually given on your type of account to pay any balance.

3. If you still are not satisfied, you should notify the creditor in writing within the time allowed to pay your bill.

Maintaining your credit rating

A creditor may not threaten your credit rating while you're resolving a billing dispute. Once you have written about a possible error, a creditor is prohibited from giving out information to other creditors or credit bureaus that would damage your credit reputation. And, until your complaint is answered, the creditor also may not take any action to collect the disputed amount.

After the creditor has explained the bill, you may be reported as delinquent on the amount in dispute, and the creditor may take action to collect if you do not pay in the time allowed. Even so, you can still disagree in writing. Then the creditor must report that you have challenged your bill and give you the name and address of each person who has received information about your account. When the matter is settled, the creditor must report the outcome to each person who has received information. Remember that you may also place your own side of the story in your credit record. (See the section on consumer statements in Chapter 9.)

Defective goods or services

Your new sofa arrives with only three legs. You try to return it; no luck. You ask the merchant to repair or replace it; still no luck. The Fair Credit Billing Act provides that you may withhold payment on any damaged or poor-quality services purchased with a credit card, as long as you have made a real attempt to solve the problem with the merchant.

This right may be limited if the card was a bank or travel-and-entertainment card or any card not issued by the store where you made your purchase. In such cases, the sale must have been for more than $50 and must have taken place in your home state or within 100 miles of your home address.

Credit for payments and refunds

If you can avoid finance charges on your account by paying within a certain period of time, it is obviously important that you receive your bills and get credit for paying them promptly. Check your statements to make sure your creditor follows these rules:

1. *Prompt billing.* Look at the date on the postmark. If your account is one on which no finance or other charge is added before a certain due date, then creditors must mail their statements at least 14 days before payment is due.
2. *Prompt crediting.* Look at the payment date entered on the statement. Creditors must credit payments on the day they arrive, as long as you follow payment instructions.
3. *Credit balances.* If a credit balance is created on your account (for example, because you pay more than the amount owed, or you return an item and the purchase price is credited to your account), the creditor must make a refund to you in cash. The refund must be made within seven business days after your written request or automatically if the credit balance is still in existence after six months.

Rules for safe credit card use

- ❑ Keep a list of your credit card numbers, expiration dates, and the telephone numbers of each card issuer in a secure place.
- ❑ When selecting a card, compare the terms offered by several card issuers to find the one that best suits your needs. Credit card issuers offer a wide variety of terms (annual percentage rate, methods of calculating the balance subject to the finance charge, minimum monthly payments, and actual membership fees).

- ❑ Watch your card after giving it to a clerk. Take it back promptly and make sure it's yours.
- ❑ Tear up the carbons when you take your credit card receipt. Void or destroy any incorrect receipts.
- ❑ Never sign a blank receipt. Draw a line through any blank spaces above the total when you sign receipts.
- ❑ Open credit card bills promptly and compare them with your receipts to check for unauthorized charges and billing errors.
- ❑ Report promptly and in writing to the card issuer any questionable charges. Check the billing statement for the correct address to send any written inquiries. The inquiry must be in writing to guarantee your rights.
- ❑ Never give out your credit card number over the telephone unless you have initiated the call.
- ❑ Never put your card number on a postcard or on the outside of an envelope.
- ❑ Sign new cards as soon as they arrive. Cut up expired cards and dispose of them promptly. Cut up and return unwanted cards to the issuer.
- ❑ Leave infrequently used cards in a secure place.
- ❑ If any of your credit cards are missing or stolen, report the loss to your card issuers as soon as possible. Some companies have 24-hour service and toll-free numbers printed on their statements for this purpose. For your own protection, follow up your phone calls with a letter to each issuer. The letter should contain your card number, the date you discovered the card was missing, and the date you reported the loss.
- ❑ If you report the loss before a credit card is used, the issuer cannot hold you responsible for any subsequent unauthorized charges. If a thief uses your card before you report it missing, the most you will owe for unauthorized charges on each card is $50.

SAMPLE LETTER: BILLING ERROR NOTIFICATION

[Your address]

[Date]

[Company name]
Credit department
[Street address]

Re: **[Account number]**

Dear Sir or Madam:

In my most recent billing statement dated **[date]**, I believe that there is an error. The statement lists a **[amount]** charge for a(n) **[item]** purchased on **[date]**. I did not make such a purchase. Please check your records again. My account number is **[account number]**, and the account is under the name of **[your name]**.

Thank you for your cooperation.

Sincerely,
[Your signature]

[Your name]

SAMPLE LETTER: DEFECTIVE MERCHANDISE

[Your address]

[Date]

[Company name]
Credit department
[Address]

Re: **[Account number]**

Dear Sir or Madam:

I purchased **[item]** on **[date]** using my Visa card. The **[item]** was defective so I returned it to the store and received a credit against my card. Today I got a bill from you indicating that I still owe money for the **[item]**, which I returned. Please delete that purchase from my bill and send me an updated bill.

Thank you for your cooperation.

Sincerely,
[Your signature]

[Your name]

SAMPLE LETTER: NOTIFICATION OF DOUBLE BILLING

[Your address]
[Date]

[Company name]
Credit department
[Address]

Re: **[Account number]**

Dear Sir or Madam:

My latest bill from your company indicates a charge of **[amount]** for a purchase I made on **[date]**. The bill also shows another charge for the exact same amount on the same date. I did not make two purchases on the date in question. Please delete the second charge from my account and send me an updated bill reflecting the correction.

Thank you for your cooperation.

Sincerely,
[Your signature]

[Your name]

Chapter 2

Late payments and debt collectors

If a creditor has received no payment by the end of the billing cycle, it considers an account delinquent. The initial contact will come in the form of a friendly reminder. This reminder is usually printed on the following month's (billing cycle's) statement or sometimes in a separate letter. Most delinquencies are paid after this reminder. Most people who fall in this category do so because they forgot, misplaced the statement, or are temporarily short of funds.

When no payment has been received during the past two billing cycles, a creditor must be careful in its approach. It wants to keep you as a customer, but it needs to collect the overdue amount. At this stage, you will receive several formal letters about 10 to 20 days apart. If no payment or response arrives, the next step is a phone call. The collection department will inform you of the seriousness of the delinquency and inquire as to when you will make a payment.

After about three months of not receiving a payment, the creditor will realize there is a serious problem with the account and will use a stronger approach. Before turning the account over to a collection agency or attorney, the creditor will make every effort to contact you and get you to pay. It realizes the longer a debt is overdue, the harder it is to collect.

Next, the company will rescind any credit you may still have available with it, and you will be advised that your account is being handed over to an agency or attorney for collection. In many cases, the firm will charge off your account and write it off as a loss. In some cases, it may have its in-house collection department pursue the debt. If the collection agency is unsuccessful and the amount owed warrants it, the account is given to an attorney for legal action.

The Fair Debt Collection Practices Act

Congress passed the Fair Debt Collection Practices Act (FDCPA) to protect consumers against harassment and other unethical practices by those who collect unpaid debts. If a debt collector contacts you on behalf of one of your creditors, you should be aware of your rights.

Under this law, debt collectors may not use any false or deceptive tactics to collect a debt or obtain information. The following are examples of conduct forbidden by debt collectors when collecting debt:

- Using a false name.
- Pretending to be a government official, attorney, or credit bureau employee.
- Falsely claiming that you have committed a crime and will be arrested.
- Claiming your wages or property will be seized, unless it is legal and the debt collector or creditor intends to seize your wages or property.
- Giving you papers that appear to be government or legal documents but are not.
- Leading you to believe that certain legal forms do not require any action on your part.
- Giving or threatening to give out false information about you.
- Threatening to take any action that cannot legally be taken or that they do not intend to take.

Debtors' rights at work

Working and debt collection don't mix. Whatever your reasons for not paying your debts, you have the right to keep your private financial affairs from becoming common office knowledge. Harassment at work or any place else is illegal. However, it's not illegal for a debt collector to call you at work—unless you tell the collector it's inconvenient for you. Any collector who calls to discuss payment of your debt after you've said not to is breaking the law.

Collectors can, however, contact you to tell you that no further collection efforts will be made or to inform you of a specific action to be taken against you. Or if the creditor has actually taken court action against you and the court has ordered that your wages be attached (garnished), your employer will have to know. Otherwise, it's no one's business but yours and the debt collector's.

Collectors can call people in your office to try to locate you. In a "locator" call, a collector may only give his or her name and the purpose of the call—to confirm your work and home addresses and home phone number. Locator calls usually can be made only once and cannot indicate that you owe money.

To further protect you, the law says that collectors cannot use postcards to reach you, and they can't use envelopes that indicate that the sender is in the debt-collection business. In fact, the FDCPA prevents debt collectors from telling your boss or co-workers you owe money, unless you or a court says it's all right or such an announcement is part of a court judgment.

If you feel you've been the victim of debt-collection harassment on the job, follow these steps:

1. Tell the caller not to telephone you or anyone at your office or job.
2. Follow up with a letter saying the same thing. It's a good idea to send the letter by certified mail with a return receipt requested. Keep a copy for your files.

3. Make a list of all calls received by you or others after that time, what was said, the general tone, how you responded, and anything else worth noting. Save any message slips from debt-collectors left for you. These will be helpful if you have to take legal action later.
4. If the calls continue, report the matter to your state and local consumer-protection offices and to the Federal Trade Commission, Debt Collection, Washington, DC 20580. You might wish to consult an attorney about taking legal action against the debt collector. If you can't afford to hire an attorney, you may qualify for free legal services from a local legal-aid program. Otherwise, your local bar association's lawyer referral service may be able to recommend a private lawyer qualified to handle your case.
5. If a debt collector violates the FDCPA, you have the right to sue for actual damages, additional damages (up to $1,000), court costs, and reasonable attorney's fees. If you sue, try to find an attorney who is willing to accept whatever the judge awards as the entire fee for representing you.

The sample cease and desist letters on pages 37 and 38 can be used or modified to stop creditors from continued harassment. Be sure to keep a copy for your files as further violations of this request may allow you to bring court action against the collector.

Appendix C includes a complete version of the Fair Debt Collection Practices Act.

Hearings and court judgments

If you have received a notice to appear in court concerning a problem with a creditor, it is definitely to your advantage to appear. A creditor must notify you at least 15 days in advance of a scheduled court date, thus allowing you an opportunity to appear and defend your rights. You have the right to a legal hearing before a creditor can have your wages garnished or your property seized.

Most creditors win judgments simply because the individuals against whom the actions are made do not show up in court. If you do appear, most courts will work with you, and they will often allow an extended period of time for you to repay the account. If you do not appear for the hearing, expect a wage garnishment to be placed in effect.

There are many cases where people have defaulted for valid reasons. Many of these reasons will hold up in court when you have a dispute against the creditor. They may include defective merchandise, negligent service, improper billing, or fraud. Under the Fair Credit Billing Act, you have the right to withhold payment in any disputed portion of a bill until the creditor resolves the dispute.

Remember, if a creditor informs you that it intends to repossess the articles in dispute, you should:

1. Seek help before you are led to legal proceedings.
2. Always appear at any scheduled hearings.
3. Seek legal assistance through an attorney or your local Legal Aid Society if you need help to defend your case.

Collection agencies

When an account is turned over for collection, the first thing the collection agency does is to notify you by mail that they are now responsible for the collection process. Once you receive notification that your account has been turned over to a collection agency you have the right to contact the agency and tell them that you want them to return the account to the credit grantor. You can make their collection efforts difficult by demanding that they provide complete verification and documentation of the debt including original signed applications and billing statements.

When the agency notifies the credit grantor of your request, the credit grantor may take your statement as an indication that you are ready to settle. They will usually accept the account back with the understanding that you will negotiate a prompt settlement. If you can negotiate a series of regular payments that will pay off the balance the credit grantor may accept that payment plan because that means they will get all the money you pay. Nothing will be kept by the collection agency. The credit grantor does not want to pay a collection agency unless it's absolutely necessary. The credit grantor's letter to you will usually demand that you send them payment in full along with a request that you contact them if there is any error in the records or objection to the charge.

Consider that possibility carefully. Is the charge legitimate? Is there an honest question that you owe the money? For example:

- ❑ Did you actually receive the material that was supposed to be delivered to you? Does the vendor have evidence that you actually took delivery? If they do not, you may challenge the obligation. (For example, did UPS deliver the package to the reception desk at your office but the package was never given to you?)
- ❑ Did you authorize this purchase? If it is a telephone or direct-mail purchase, was your name, credit card, or job title used without your approval?
- ❑ Did a relative charge your child's medical expense to you without your approval? Or did your child use your credit without approval? Did your spouse use your credit after you notified the credit grantor that you two were legally separated or divorced?

Collecting damages

Even though you may owe money to a credit grantor or to a collection agency, you still have the protection of specific legal rights. If they are violated you have the right to protect yourself. You can collect damages from abusive creditors if they violate the Fair Debt Collection Practices Act in trying to collect money from you. A couple in Texas was awarded $11 million from a collection agency that used excessive harassment in trying to collect a $1,000 credit card debt.

Even a minor technical violation of the law can draw severe penalties. A debt collector found guilty of even a minor violation may be ordered to pay damages, which can include action and statutory damages, attorneys' fees and costs, and—in some cases—additional damages (i.e., a penalty payment intended to teach the violator a lesson). The protection of the law includes not only the debtor but also others who might have been affected by violations, such as relatives, friends, co-workers, and employers.

These laws are not widely understood and different judges handle similar cases in different ways—there is not enough common experience that tends to standardize the enforcement process. One court may hold that multiple violations are all part of a single collection effort and lump the findings together, while a second court may separate each act in violation to become a separate court charge.

You may receive compensation for out-of-pocket expenses, emotional distress and mental anguish, loss of reputation (with family, co-workers, or neighbors), and other damages, as well as recovery of legal fees and costs incurred by a debtor protecting his or her interests. Because recovery of legal fees is specifically included in this law, more and more attorneys are willing to accept these cases on a contingency fee arrangement.

Documentation and accurate records

Documentation—and the discipline of accumulating good documentation—can be your best ally in the process of working with collectors and keeping them from harassing you.

Organize a file folder for each account that is in collection and discipline yourself to put every piece of paper that applies to this account in that folder and to establish a record of all telephone contacts. Never write on the original copy of any document. You always want these originals to be clean and free of notes that may become confusing in the future.

Staple a clean sheet of lined paper inside the folder and record every telephone conversation on this sheet. Note and date every phone contact (inbound and outbound) and identify in detail to whom you're speaking (using full names, telephone extension numbers, and employee ID numbers to clearly identify each person accurately). Clearly indicate what was discussed and what was agreed. If any follow-up is required, be sure to post a note in your personal calendar reminding you what action was to be accomplished by this date.

This simple tracking system will provide you with a detailed history of every contact, action, and agreement between you and the creditor. This may become excellent evidence in a court action.

3 dynamic negotiation strategies

These three strategies will help you resolve any collection action in a way that is either positive or neutral in your credit files:

1. Be absolutely sure that this debt is really yours and is properly documented. You cannot be penalized for failure to pay a charge that is not yours, that you have not authorized, for which you have no legal liability, or that the vendor cannot properly document.
2. Attempt to satisfy legitimate debts with the fewest dollars out of pocket, paid over the longest term.
3. Never agree to a payment plan that does not include protection against negative entries on your report.

Once you are engaged in the negotiation process, base every discussion with the collector on the "if...then..." relationship—"If I do this, then you will do that."

Strategies for medical debts

One accident or serious illness can ruin you financially for life. It's imperative to understand how hospitals deal with their accounts receivable. Because hospitals are on tight budgets, they must turn their receivables into cash as quickly as possible. They do this by selling your account to companies (called factors) at a discount. If the total receivables for one month are $200,000, for instance, a factor may purchase them for $175,000. The factor then attempts to collect the entire $200,000 and make a profit.

Whether or not your insurance company is paying for your treatment, always check every item on every bill and make sure you recognize the service or product as being yours. And, above all, look for double entries. This may not necessarily be deliberate double billing, however, as many individuals contribute input to your invoice, and only you have the last chance for correction. Demand an audit of your account if you suspect error.

When you receive medical bills, don't think that just because an amount is on your bill, that the amount is necessarily fair. Medical facilities use a standard schedule of fees to determine approximately how long a procedure will take and how much to charge. They use those schedules as a beginning point to charge. The same procedure could be twice the price just a mile down the road. The amount you are charged may differ based upon where you live.

Don't be afraid to challenge suspected overcharges. You may be amazed to learn that most healthcare providers don't always demand to receive the full amount they charge and are often willing to negotiate. You have a right to see their schedule of fees. Ask for it and begin negotiating.

When you challenge your bills, you must do so in writing and by certified mail. A paper trail is a necessity for proving your case should future problems arise concerning your bill.

Strategies for student loans

Colleges, universities, and trade schools market student loans as aggressively as any bank or credit card company. One difference, though, that separates higher-education loans from most other private-sector loans: The federal government guarantees student loans.

This means that if the student defaults, the educational institution has already been paid and the government pays off the lender. There is no risk on the part of the lender or the institution when the government guarantees the loan. So there is little, if any, incentive on the part of the lender or institution to properly qualify the borrower. As a result, certain schools have been established to get as many students as possible to obtain student loans. When enough cash has poured in, the owners abscond with the loot. If this happened at an institution you attended, you may have an argument not to pay the loan.

The downside of defaulting on a student loan is that they are not generally dischargeable under bankruptcy and the IRS can withhold refunds until the loan has been paid in full.

If you have a student loan that has gone to collection, the first step is to send a cease and desist letter to the collection agency. Then begin negotiating with the original lender. Request a moratorium (also known as a forbearance) on your payments. You may get as much as three years' deferral. Interest will not be accrued during this period. Student loan deferrals may be given due to illness, job loss, military duty, or a return to school.

If you're still in trouble after your deferment, get in touch with the Department of Education at (800) 433-3243 and let the Debt Collection Department know your situation. Follow up your call with a written version of the conversation and keep references of everyone you talk to, noting the times and dates. The record of your contact may be needed as a defense should your debt go to the IRS.

If you attended trade school or an institution that collapsed before you graduated or received your training, and you still owe the loan, you have a good argument to refuse to pay the loan and to have the negative information deleted from your credit report. After all, the government has the responsibility to regulate the institutions that are taking advantage of those guaranteed student loans.

SAMPLE LETTER: TO END COMMUNICATION

[Your address]
[Date]

[Collection company]
[Address]

Dear Sir or Madam:

As I discussed with you on the telephone last week, I maintain that I do not owe the alleged debt to **[name of creditor]**. Therefore, I wish to end all communication with you, any of your employees, or anyone hired by your company in regard to this alleged debt.

Sincerely,
[Your signature]

[Your name]

SAMPLE LETTER: CEASE AND DESIST

[Your address]
[Date]

[Collection company]
[Address]

Re: **[Statement of debt]**

Dear Sir or Madam:

Under to the Fair Debt Collection Practices Act, I have the right to demand that you cease and desist all further communication with me. I hereby give official notice to your firm to stop your attempts to contact me in any manner regarding the above debt. I would prefer to resolve this problem with the original company with whom I have contracted.

A copy of this letter will also be sent to the Federal Trade Commission, State Attorney General, and the Better Business Bureau if you do not immediately honor this formal cease and desist request.

Sincerely,
[Your signature]

[Your name]

Chapter 3

Guerrilla tactics for rapid debt reduction

The following is a list of tactics that will allow you to break out of the cycle of increasing debt quickly:

- ❑ Practice abstinence by not incurring additional unsecured debt. (Unsecured debt is any debt that is not secured by some type of collateral, such as a car, house, etc.) Begin by taking all of your credit cards out of your wallet and putting them in a safe place. (The safest place is cut up into little pieces in an envelope en route to the companies that issued them.)
- ❑ Join a support group, such as Debtors Anonymous, and attend meetings on a regular basis. Here you can learn how others overcame their problems with debt and share their experiences, strength, and hope.
- ❑ Contact the nearest office of Consumer Credit Counselors and ask for help in developing a repayment plan. They can assist you in drawing up a budget and arranging more lenient repayment schedules.

- ❑ Maintain records of daily expenses and of the retirement of any portions of your outstanding debts. This will help you clarify spending patterns.
- ❑ Make a list of all of the people you owe and arrange to complete your agreements with them all.
- ❑ Reduce your outstanding debts to a minimum. Start by paying off the accounts with the lowest balances. Pay off all of your existing debts by making accelerated payments.
- ❑ Find a way to increase your income. This can be done by renting out a room in your home, finding another job, or starting a profitable sideline that requires little start-up capital and minimum overhead (such as housecleaning, a home-based word-processing service, babysitting, etc.).
- ❑ Maintain awareness of the credit system by taking note of bank, loan company, and credit card advertising and by reading news accounts of its effects. Educate yourself by reading other books on consumer credit. Know your rights!

Creative auto financing

Before road testing the latest models, do your homework. Determine the payments you can afford based on your present budget. Then decide on the type of car that fits your particular needs as well as your pocketbook.

One suggestion is to take the monthly payment you expect to pay on the new car and put it in your savings account for six months. See if you can handle the payments; if you can with no problem, use what you've saved as the down payment.

You should also try to sell your present vehicle yourself. You can often get much more for it than the dealer will give you. However, do not keep your old car after the day you buy the new one, even if the dealer isn't going to give you the amount you think it is worth. It is more important to lower the amount you must borrow on the new car than it is to get the most you can for the old one.

In financing your new car, be sure that the credit plan allows for early payoff without penalty. Most manufacturers' finance plans are relatively inflexible. They can even have hidden penalties for early payoff or any modification of your terms. Always keep in mind that no matter how low the manufacturer's advertised interest rate is, you will always get a better deal if you can pay cash.

Use all your trade-in money and as much cash as you can come up with as your down payment. Use all the dealer-incentive money you can get and go to your bank or credit union for your financing. Tell your bank representative that your purpose is to pay off your loan as rapidly as possible. Insist that your loan terms allow early payoff. Ask if it is possible to borrow the entire amount you plan to finance for 90 days, promising to refinance the balance into a monthly payment plan at the end of that time.

This time allows you to add as much as you can to your down payment. During this period, work as much overtime as possible, have garage sales, or sell unnecessary assets to gather more cash. The whole family can get involved in a 90-day pay-down marathon. If everyone pitches in, it's possible to lower the financed amount by as much as one-half.

Any additional down-payment money you make during this time should be paid to the bank as soon as you get it. Every cent you pay during this period lowers your interest cost from that day on. At the end of that time, refinance the remaining balance for the shortest time possible.

Rapid mortgage reduction

One simple way to reduce the balance on your mortgage is to make the first loan payment on the day you take out the loan. If the first payment is made on the day the loan is made, many months, and possibly even several years, can be reduced from the total length of your mortgage.

Here's how it works. In the first years of the mortgage, only a very small percentage of your monthly payment goes toward the principal. The majority of your payment goes toward paying interest. If the first payment is made on the day you make your loan, there is no interest due at that time. The entire payment will be subtracted from the principal of the loan.

Another way to pay off your mortgage rapidly is to make a payment every week. To figure the amount that each weekly payment should be, multiply your monthly payment by 12 (months in a year), then divide that amount by 52 (weeks in a year). The answer will give you the amount your weekly payment should be.

Let's say, for example, that your mortgage payment is $866.67 per month. If you multiply that by 12 months, you have the amount of your total annual mortgage payment. Your answer will be $10,400. Now divide $10,400 by 52 weeks. Your answer will be $200. If you then pay $200 each week, you will drastically lower the amount of interest you owe.

Each week you will be lowering the principal and interest by a small amount. At first it won't seem like you're accomplishing much, but by the time several years have passed, the savings will become more significant. The interest on a mortgage that is paid off weekly will be lowered by as much as 60 percent when compared to a similar mortgage that is paid off with monthly payments. Not only will the total interest cost be less, but the time it takes to pay off the mortgage will be drastically reduced if this procedure is followed faithfully.

Another alternative is to make a half-payment every 14 days. This will result in making one extra payment each year and will take years off the length of time it takes to pay off the balance of your mortgage. If a half-payment is made every two weeks, you will make 26 half-payments each year. Fifty-two weeks divided by two weeks equals 26 weeks. Divide the 26 half-payments by two, and you have 13 full payments instead of the 12 you would make if you paid one full payment each month.

These suggestions are all mathematically sound methods of rapid mortgage reduction. But remember that your lender must approve any modification made to an existing mortgage. The mortgage holder is not obligated to do anything that is not expressly stated in the loan agreement that you both signed. It is best to make these types of arrangements before you take out the mortgage. However, many lenders will agree to modify your payment schedule if you ask.

The truth about debt consolidation

A consolidation loan will rarely reduce the amount of money you owe. There will be new loan costs added to your balance. Your interest will also go up because you will be taking much longer to pay off the new loan. Consolidation-borrowing almost always adds to your debt. In other words, you can't borrow your way out of debt.

Let's imagine that your current bills total $10,000, and it will take five years to pay off a consolidation loan at a payment of $265 per month. With this loan structure, your new debt, with interest, equals $15,900.

The act of debt consolidation usually results in a somewhat lower monthly payment, but this payment must be made for a much longer period of time. For example, you could also consolidate that same $10,000 debt so that your payments would drop to half the $265 we used in the previous illustration. This would make your new payment only $132.50 per month.

Sounds great, doesn't it? Think about it, though. The term of the lower monthly payment will now be 12 years instead of five years. So, your true total debt will go up to $19,080.

Consolidation by a bank or finance company usually will not reduce your total cost in terms of time served to pay off your debt. These institutions almost always charge a higher interest rate because your risk of default or bankruptcy has increased since you made the original loans.

Debt consolidation is simply another method of enslaving you in further debt. The lender is the one who benefits, not the borrower. Debt consolidation is done for three basic reasons:

1. It discourages bankruptcies.
2. It gives the lender a chance to adjust the interest rate upward.
3. The lender has the opportunity to add collateral to the loan.

Once again, you can't borrow your way out of debt—no matter what the commercials might lead you to believe. You can only borrow your way deeper into debt. The only exception is if you can get the interest on your total bill reduced. The debt would be paid off more quickly because more of each payment will be going toward paying off the balance of your loan. Usually the only circumstance in which this can happen is when you owe large amounts of high-interest credit card debts. They can sometimes be consolidated into a second mortgage on your home, which usually carries a lower interest rate. This type of loan can also have the additional advantage of being tax deductible.

Last-resort strategies

If you feel your back is to the wall but not quite enough to file bankruptcy, propose a more favorable alternative to your creditors. You can often obtain many favorable terms by simply threatening to file bankruptcy. The credit manager who was on your back will suddenly become a model of generosity, offering temporary collection moratoria, extended payments—anything at all to get more return on the credit his company extended than what the bankruptcy court will give him. Ask for a debt moratorium to help you get back on your feet and resume payments at a later time, or suggest reducing payments to an amount you can reasonably handle. The cost of fighting a bankruptcy petition, along with the near certainty of having little or nothing to show for it, should make most creditors ready to agree to your proposal.

SAMPLE LETTER: TO REQUEST A MORATORIUM I

[Your address]
[Date]

[Company name]
[Address]

RE: [Account and amount due]

Dear Credit Manager:

After a careful review of my financial situation, I find that it is impossible for me to meet the scheduled monthly payments on my account due to **[special reason for present hardship, e.g., emergency expenses, large medical bills, unemployment]**.

After deducting my carefully budgeted living expenses from my current monthly income, the balance is simply inadequate to pay my debts at the present rate. Therefore, I propose that my payments be reduced to $**[amount]** next year, unless the debt is paid off sooner.

Your cooperation will be of considerable help in avoiding the alternative of bankruptcy.

Sincerely,

[Your signature]

[Your name]

SAMPLE LETTER: TO REQUEST A MORATORIUM II

[Your address]
[Date]

[Company name]
[Address]

RE: [Account and amount due]

Dear Credit Manager:

After a careful review of my financial condition, I find it impossible for me to meet the scheduled monthly payments due to **[reason for present hardship]**.

After deducting my carefully budgeted living expenses from my current monthly income, the balance is simply inadequate to pay my debts at the present rate. Therefore, I propose a **[number]**-month moratorium on my repayment of my debt. At the end of that period, I hope to resume monthly payments of $**[amount]** per month, for at least **[number]** months.

Your cooperation will be of considerable help in avoiding the alternative of bankruptcy.

Sincerely,

[Your signature]

[Your name]

SAMPLE LETTER: TO REQUEST REDUCED PAYMENTS

[Your address]
[Date]

[Company name]
[Address]

RE: [Account number]

Dear Credit Manager:

If you check my account, you will find it to be delinquent. This is due to **[reason for delinquent account]**.

I would like to have your consent to a repayment plan that is manageable for me. My present balance is $**[amount]**. With your consent, I will send you a payment of $**[amount]** each month, starting **[date]**. Payment in full would be in approximately **[number]** months instead of the present **[number]** months. I foresee no circumstances that would prevent me from making these payments. A check in the amount of $**[amount]** is enclosed. Please notify me if you find these terms acceptable, and I will come in to sign a contract.

Thank you for your patience and confidence. I will increase my payments whenever my budget allows.

Sincerely yours,

[Your signature]

[Your name]

Chapter 4

Going bankrupt without going broke

After 12 years of marriage, Jennifer's husband disappeared, leaving her to care for five children. He also left her with $63,000 in outstanding loans and mortgage payments. After two years of trying to make ends meet, Jennifer sought protection under Chapter 7 of the bankruptcy code.

"Filing bankruptcy seemed like my only way out," Jennifer said. "I tried to establish credit and pay off my bills by myself, but I just couldn't make it. When my husband left and stopped making child-support payments, I just couldn't do it anymore."

People who file for bankruptcy are usually struggling to get by with the basic necessities of life. They are not living lavishly, running up big bills, and then filing for bankruptcy to avoid responsibility. If income is disrupted for any length of time because of injury, sickness, or layoff, even the most comfortable among us can suddenly find ourselves swimming in a sea of credit card debts, medical bills, and overdue rent or mortgage payments. For some people, bankruptcy can offer a fresh start in life.

The Bankruptcy Act is a federal law that is intended to benefit both troubled debtors and their creditors. One purpose is to make sure the debtor's property is equitably distributed to the creditors so no creditor will have an unfair advantage over the others.

The law also provides the honest debtor with protection against his creditors' demands for payment. If the debtor makes a full and honest accounting of his assets and liabilities and deals fairly with the creditors, he may have most, if not all, of his debts discharged or cancelled. The bankruptcy process is intended to give the debtor a new beginning without the burden of unmanageable debts.

The tradition of debt relief dates back to the time of Moses. To protect the poor, a provision of the Year of Jubilee, celebrated every 50 years, was the cancellation of all private debts incurred by the Israelites. For example, Israelites whose debts had caused them to be sold as slaves were released from debts and given their liberty.

Bankruptcy statutes have been around in England since 1542. The U.S. Constitution provides for bankruptcy legislation. The Bankruptcy Act of 1898 formed the basis of U.S. laws for many years. Congress completely revised the act in 1978 and added further amendments in 1984.

There are basically two types of bankruptcy protection for the individual consumer: Chapter 7 liquidation and Chapter 13 debt adjustment.

Chapter 7 liquidation

Chapter 7 liquidation, sometimes referred to as straight bankruptcy, is the most common form of bankruptcy filed by debtors.

Under Chapter 7, most of your debts will be discharged by the court, and you will never have to repay them. However, certain debts are not dischargeable and will survive bankruptcy. For example, certain income taxes that accrue prior to the filing of a petition and obligations to pay alimony and child support are not dischargeable. You should consult your attorney as to what kinds of debts are dischargeable in your particular case.

The primary purpose of this kind of bankruptcy is to give an honest debtor a fresh start in life without the pressure and discouragement of substantial indebtedness. The result is complete forgiveness of all debts and a chance to rebuild one's life.

Another feature of bankruptcy protection is the automatic stay. An automatic stay requires creditors to immediately stop all efforts to collect a debt, take possession of collateral, enforce a lien, set off a debt, or collect receivables. The creditor must request any relief from these restrictions from the bankruptcy court.

Disadvantages of Chapter 7

Chapter 7 bankruptcy is not a panacea for everyone with financial difficulties. It has its limitations, which include:

1. *Frequency.* It cannot be filed again within the next six years.
2. *Disposition of assets.* Upon filing the bankruptcy petition, the property belonging to the debtor, with the exception of certain property exempted under federal or state laws, becomes part of the debtor's estate to be liquidated for distribution to creditors. Therefore, the loss of assets must be considered when contemplating the filing of a petition.

Chapter 13 debt adjustment

An alternative to Chapter 7 liquidation is Chapter 13 debt adjustment. Formerly known as the "Wage Earner Plan," Chapter 13 is designed to enable individual debtors to apply a portion of their debts over an extended period of time. This is done under court supervision and through a court-appointed trustee. The debtor is protected from the creditors by an automatic stay while a plan of repayment is developed and carried out.

The underlying policy is to encourage debtors to pay their debts instead of merely seeking a discharge. Therefore, the justification of pursuing Chapter 13 relief instead of liquidation is one of moral consideration. For many debtors, however, this sense of morality often creates a difficult course to pursue because of the need to support dependents while being burdened by the repayment of heavy debts. Many who file under Chapter 13 with good intentions can never follow through with the payment plan and finally abandon it. As a result, the case is dismissed under the petition of the trustee or converted to Chapter 7.

Advantages of Chapter 13

1. Chapter 13 protects the debtor's nonexempt assets, which would be lost in a liquidation case. Thus, it is important for you to consult an attorney and determine the extent of your property that is nonexempt and its value.
2. If there are substantial nondischargeable debts, such as spousal support, student loans, or willful and malicious injury to property, Chapter 13 allows you to eliminate, reduce, or pay such debts over an extended period of time. In contrast, a Chapter 7 liquidation would not protect the debtor from enforcement of these nondischargeable obligations.
3. Chapter 13 is available to individuals who may not be eligible for a Chapter 7 discharge. For example, a person who received a discharge under Chapter 7 within the past six years can't obtain another discharge, but may seek relief and receive one under Chapter 13.
4. A debtor's personal sense of morality may compel him to file under Chapter 13 and lessen the sense of guilt. Chapter 13 allows an individual to maintain a sense of integrity.
5. Future creditors may look favorably upon a person who, despite past financial failures, has attempted to repay his/her debts in an honest and ethical way.
6. The new Chapter 13 code contains a special automatic stay provision applicable to co-debtors or cosigners.

After the filing of a Chapter 13 case, a creditor may not act on, commence, or continue any civil action to collect all or any part of the debt from any individual who is liable with the debtor. The stay also protects any individuals who put up collateral to secure the debt. However, it is important to understand that this stay would not affect the substantive rights of the lender with respect to the cosigner's liability. All it does is require the lender to wait for payment under the Chapter 13 plan before pursuing remedies against the co-debtor.

7. The filing of Chapter 13 stops interest charges on your accounts.

Proposed reforms

In 1978, less than 200,000 consumers filed bankruptcy—about one per every 400 households. In 1998, there were a record number of more than 1.4 million filings—approximately one for every 70 households. More consumers filed bankruptcy during the first six months of 1999 than during the entire decade of the Depression. As a result of this dramatic rise in bankruptcy filings, credit card companies, retailers, and other lenders have begun calling for stricter bankruptcy laws. Opposing reform were women's groups, consumer advocates, and bankruptcy lawyers, who blamed aggressive marketing practices by credit card companies for the sharp increase.

The Bankruptcy Reform Act of 1998 died in committee at the close of the 105th Congress under threat of presidential veto. The act would have imposed strict-means testing on consumers by allowing judges to either dismiss a Chapter 7 case or convert it to a Chapter 13 repayment plan. Debtors would have to earn less than the national median income for their household size (i.e., $51,400 for a family of four) or have less than $50 per month left over after living expenses and obligations like child support and back taxes. Here are some of the provisions included under the proposed reforms:

- Creditors will be given 90 days, instead of 30, to contest claims.
- Only debtors who can't pay all of their secured debts (i.e., mortgages and car loans), priority obligations (child support, alimony, and unpaid taxes), and at least 20% of their unsecured debts would have the option of filing for complete relief under Chapter 7. Otherwise, debtors must file under Chapter 13 and repay their debts.
- The period between Chapter 7 discharges would be extended from six to eight years.
- Debts incurred within 90 days of filing would be nondischargeable.

People from all walks of life have had to opt for filing bankruptcy. What do you do when you have to choose between your creditors and your family? Sometimes bankruptcy is the best option—sometimes it is the only option. A general rule of thumb is that if your total unsecured debts total twice your annual income—and you don't foresee an improvement to your financial circumstances—you may need to consider bankruptcy as an option. If you do take this route, it doesn't necessarily mean the end of one's financial life. Here are some more stories to illustrate that there is, in fact, life after debt.

Tamara and her husband, John, opened a restaurant catering to upscale customers in the entertainment industry. John had experience in the restaurant industry and had researched the market well, so they had big dreams of success.

As partners, Tamara and John agreed to invest an equal amount in the business. Tamara's half came from her grandmother in Oregon, who was entering a retirement home. Quite wealthy at the time, her grandmother agreed to sell her home and give Tamara the proceeds for her stake in the restaurant. John told Tamara his half would come from a friend in Texas, a silent partner.

The restaurant opened with great fanfare and did well for several months. However, as Tamara recalls, "We were overstaffed and undercapitalized. Most celebrities opted for trendier establishments. After a year or so, we had to borrow money to stay afloat. We used our personal friends, and even my parents and an uncle signed personal notes."

Eventually Tamara realized that John had not invested any money in the business. "No wonder we were having problems," she lamented. "We just went broke and filed bankruptcy. The bank that owned our fixtures advised us to hold a bankruptcy sale. Our employees were loyal to the end and even offered to work without paychecks.

"It seems everything fell apart at the same time, including my marriage. I know the marriage could have worked out if it hadn't been for the bankruptcy. John was so depressed he could hardly function. His dream had been destroyed, and he couldn't cope with the consequences. I felt sorry for him, but I also felt betrayed because he never put money of his own into the business."

Tamara says that many of their so-called friends regarded them as "deadbeats" and no longer wanted to associate with them. Their children were ridiculed at school. Tamara couldn't get credit anywhere and even had trouble getting a check cashed.

Tamara managed to pay off the loans guaranteed by her parents and her uncle. However, family members, including her mother, treated her coolly. Since Tamara's grandmother spent her final years (and her fortune) in a retirement home, Tamara was the only family member to get any of her money. And it was all gone.

With children to support and educate, Tamara's life was difficult. But she was determined not to let these reverses ruin their lives. She went back to work and, with the help of a financial counselor, reestablished her credit.

Today she is the president of her own consulting firm. Her work brings her in contact with people having financial problems. "They often say to me, 'You just don't know what it's like to be so heavily in debt.'

"Oh yes, I do," Tamara assures them, "but there is life after debt."

Jack had been a successful Hollywood screenwriter for nearly a decade and was used to lavish living and expensive cars. But he hadn't sold a script for more than two years. Now creditors were hounding him, his house was in foreclosure, and he was a year behind in child support and alimony payments. He was even forced to take a job making coffee at the local Starbucks just to survive. After getting a bill from the IRS for $75,000 in unpaid taxes, Jack sought the advice of an attorney. He was advised to file Chapter 13 bankruptcy. This would protect him from imminent foreclosure and repossession. It would also stall off the IRS and allow him to develop a court-supervised repayment plan. Although he still ended up losing his house and moving into a small apartment, he did manage to keep his car, office equipment, and other important necessities. He was able to begin making modest payments toward child support, alimony, and back taxes. Seven months into the debt repayment plan, Jack sold a screenplay for $250,000 and was able to pay off his debts and dismiss the bankruptcy altogether. He still maintains a modest apartment in Los Angeles and promises not to live above his means in the future.

Part 2

A do-it-yourself guide to credit repair

Chapter 5
Credit-reporting agencies

When his wife filed for divorce, David was left with mountains of bills, including an overdue student loan. His car payment was two months late, and his checking account was $700 overdrawn. Creditors threatened to sue and attach his wages.

On the advice of his attorney, David filed for protection under Chapter 13 of the bankruptcy code. The automatic stay gave him enough breathing room to begin getting his life back in order.

Three years later, David completed his debt repayment plan and was ready to start over again in the credit world. Much wiser now, he knew that he would never make the same mistakes he had made before. With a good job and steady income, David decided that it was time to purchase a new car. The 1978 Volvo he had been driving was costing him more money in repairs than he would be paying for a new car loan. To his surprise and humiliation, David was denied credit at every place he applied.

One of the car dealers referred David to a credit-repair company. The company promised that for $700 it would erase the negative information from his credit file and help him rebuild his credit rating. Three months after paying to have his credit restored, David discovered the company had disappeared. His credit rating remained the same. He had *been one of thousands of victims who had been lured into the trap of easy answers and promises that are too good to be true.*

For years, the Federal Trade Commission, Better Business Bureau, Consumer Credit Counselors, and Associated Credit Bureaus, Inc. have warned consumers to be aware of unscrupulous operators in the credit-repair industry. Despite such efforts, however, consumers have consistently beaten a pathway to the door of every new credit-repair company that has emerged. The fees for these services often range from $100 to $1,200. The biggest complaint from consumers is that they receive little or no results from these companies, which sometimes go out of business within a few months.

For a comprehensive inside look at the credit-repair industry, including a detailed description of various techniques for "erasing bad credit," read *Repair Your Own Credit* (Career Press).

Credit ratings

As you know, we live in a credit-oriented society. Most stores won't even accept a personal check without a major credit card to back it up. It is almost impossible to buy a house or a car without obtaining some type of financing. Even renting an apartment requires good credit these days.

Negative information in your credit files, such as previous late payments, collection accounts, or judgments, can prevent a lender from even considering your credit application—regardless of your ability to pay. In other cases, it can result in higher interest rates and extra finance charges (known as "points"). This can mean a difference of several thousand dollars on a large credit purchase, such as a new car or home.

In light of this reality, it is imperative that you begin now to improve your credit rating. If you're like 70 percent of American consumers, you probably have at least one item of negative information in your credit bureau files. In many cases, the information is incorrect, misleading, inaccurate, or obsolete. Perhaps your file contains information about someone else with a similar name or Social Security number.

Credit bureaus, also known as credit-reporting agencies, make money by compiling and selling information about you that has been reported to them by subscribers. These subscribers include banks, department stores, finance companies, collection agencies, and mortgage companies. The information includes credit histories, account balances, and payment patterns.

The credit bureaus also receive and report information found in public records. This includes bankruptcies, judgments, tax liens, wage garnishments, and notices of default. Public-record information is generally gathered manually, which can lead to inaccurate information being reported in your file.

Positive, neutral, and negative notations

The information in your credit report can be divided into three types of ratings: positive, neutral, and negative. The following are the only statements that are considered positive:

- Paid satisfactorily or paid as agreed.
- Current account with no late payments.
- Account/credit line closed at consumer's request.

The following notations are considered neutral, but in reality, anything less than a positive rating is considered negative by many credit grantors:

- Paid, was 30 days late.
- Current, was 30 days late.
- Inquiry.
- Credit card lost.
- Refinance.
- Settled.
- Paid.

The following are considered negative:

- ❑ Bankruptcy—Chapter 7 or Chapter 13.
- ❑ Judgments.
- ❑ Tax liens.
- ❑ Account closed—grantor's request.
- ❑ Paid, was 60, 90, or 120 days late.
- ❑ SCNL (subscriber cannot locate).
- ❑ Paid, collection.
- ❑ Paid, charge-off.
- ❑ Bk liq reo (bankruptcy liquidation).
- ❑ Charge-off.
- ❑ Collection account.
- ❑ Delinquent.
- ❑ Current, was 60, 90, or 120 days late.
- ❑ CHECKPOINT, TRANS ALERT, or CAUTION (potential fraud indicators).
- ❑ Excessive inquiries (looks like you've been turned down by everyone else).

The three largest credit bureaus

The following is a list of the three largest credit bureaus in the United States. Together they maintain more than 150 million individual credit records.

The cost for your credit report from the following bureaus varies from state to state, but the fee may not exceed $8. You may receive a free credit report if you have been denied credit within the last 60 days based on information supplied by that particular bureau. Include your full name, address, Social Security number, year of birth, and a photocopy of a billing statement, utility bill, driver's license, or other document that links the name of the consumer requesting the report with the address the report should be mailed to when requesting a report (whether it's complimentary or not).

- ❏ Experian (formerly TRW)
  P.O. Box 949
  Allen, TX 75013-0949
  (888) EXPERIAN (397-3742)
  `www.experian.com`
- ❏ Trans Union
  P.O. Box 390
  Springfield, PA 19064
  (800) 916-8800
  `www.transunion.com`
- ❏ Equifax
  P.O. Box 105873
  Atlanta, GA 30348
  (800) 685-1111
  `www.equifax.com`

Experian will provide consumers with one free credit report per year. Be sure to include the same information that you would for the other requested reports. Contact:

Experian Complimentary Report
P.O. Box 2350
Chatsworth, CA 91313
(800) 392-1122

Your local credit bureaus can be located through the yellow pages under "Credit Bureaus" or "Credit Reporting Agencies." You may also contact the industry's trade organization:

Associated Credit Bureaus, Inc.
16211 Park Place 10
P.O. Box 218300
Houston, TX 77218
(713) 878-1990

Questions and answers about credit-reporting agencies

Q: What is a credit-reporting agency?

A: A credit-reporting agency is commonly called a credit bureau. A credit bureau is a business organization that puts together a report about your past credit performance, keeps the information up to date, and, for a fee, furnishes the information in the form of credit reports to merchants, credit card issuers, insurance companies, and potential employers.

Q: Do I have the right to know what is in my credit file?

A: Under the FCRA, consumers have the right to know what is in their credit files at credit bureaus.

Q: What type of information is contained in my credit file?

A: Your credit file contains several types of information:

- ❑ Identifying information, such as your name, address, and Social Security number.
- ❑ Information concerning your current employment, such as the position you hold, the length of your employment, and your income.
- ❑ Information about your personal history, such as your date of birth, number of dependents, previous addresses, and previous employment.
- ❑ Information about your credit history, such as how promptly you made payments to previous creditors.
- ❑ Information about you that is available publicly, such as records of arrests, indictments, convictions, lawsuits, tax liens, marriages, bankruptcies, and court judgments.

Q: Who may obtain a copy of my credit file?

A: Only someone with a legitimate business need may see your credit file. Your credit file may be disclosed only to someone the credit bureau believes will use the information for one or more of the following purposes:

- ❏ Granting you credit, reviewing your account, or collecting on your account.
- ❏ Considering you for possible employment.
- ❏ Considering you for an insurance policy.
- ❏ Deciding whether or not you are eligible for a license or other government-related benefits, which by law require consideration of your financial responsibility or status. A credit bureau may also disclose "identifying" information, such as your name, address, places of employment, and former places of employment, to a government agent.
- ❏ Furnishing information for a business transaction between you and another person, such as renting an apartment, as long as the person requesting the report has a legitimate need for the information.
- ❏ Responding to a court order.
- ❏ Responding to an Internal Revenue Service (IRS) subpoena (with IRS notification and ample time for you to challenge the subpoena).
- ❏ Your credit file may also be disclosed to someone if you give your written permission to the credit bureau to disclose your file to that person.

Q: Why should I care about the information in my credit file?

A: The information contained in your credit file often determines whether or not you will be granted credit. It may also be used by insurance companies to decide whether to insure you or to set your insurance rate. Often, incorrect information is entered in your file, and if this occurs, you would want to have it removed.

Q: How can I find out what information is in my credit file?

A: If you applied for credit and were rejected, were denied insurance, or the cost of the insurance increased based on information contained in a credit report, the creditor denying you credit or insurance is required by law to supply you with the name and address of the credit bureau that supplied the report.

The credit bureau is required to disclose the information it has about you free of charge if you ask for the disclosure within 60 days of being notified of your credit or insurance denial. You can get in touch with the credit bureau either in person, by letter, or by telephone to learn what is in your credit file.

If you are simply curious to know what is in your file, contact all three of the major bureaus. For contact information, refer to page 62 of this chapter.

Q: What is an investigative report, and how is it different from a credit report?

A: An investigative report differs from a standard credit report in two ways:

1. It contains a different kind of information. While a credit report contains information relating to your credit history, an investigative report deals with matters of a more personal nature, such as your character, general reputation, and lifestyle.
2. The information is gathered differently. The information in an investigative report comes from personal interviews with your friends, associates, and neighbors, while information in a credit report is obtained directly from the credit bureau and from public records.

Q: What are investigative reports used for?

A: Investigative reports are used mostly by insurance companies and potential employers. Insurance companies use them in helping to decide if you are a good insurance risk. Potential employers may use them to help decide whether they want to hire you. Your current employer may use them to help in deciding on promotions.

Q: Does the law provide penalties for someone who willfully obtains information from a credit bureau under false pretenses?

A: Yes. Anyone willfully obtaining information from a credit-reporting agency under false pretenses is subject to a maximum criminal free of $5,000, a maximum of one year in prison, or both.

Q: Does the law provide any penalties for officers or employees of credit-reporting agencies who willfully provide information from the agency's files to an unauthorized person?

A: Yes. The penalties are the same as above.

Q: Do I have to give my permission before an investigative report can be made about me?

A: No, but the person who requests an investigative report has five days to notify you that an investigative report has been ordered. You have no right, however, to be informed that a report has been ordered if it is to be used for employment positions for which you have not specifically applied.

Q: Can I find out what information is in my investigative file?

A: Yes. You are entitled to know the "nature and substance" of all information in your investigative file. You are not entitled to know the source of information if the information was gathered only for use in preparing an investigative report and used for no other purpose. You are also entitled to know who has received investigative reports about you within the past six months, or within the last two years if the report was made for employment purposes.

Q: If a consumer believes a credit bureau has violated the law but does not want to sue, can he complain to someone?

A: Yes. A consumer can file a complaint with the Federal Trade Commission, state attorney general's office, or local district attorney's office.

SAMPLE LETTER: REQUEST FOR CREDIT REPORT (AFTER DENIAL)

[Your address]
[Date]

[Credit Bureau]
[Address]

To whom it may concern:

I have been denied credit within the past 60 days based on a credit report from your company. Enclosed is a copy of the denial letter. Please send me a copy of my credit report as soon as possible.

[Name]
[Present address]
[Previous address]
[Social Security number]
[Date of birth]

Thank you very much for your immediate attention.

Sincerely yours,
[Your signature]

[Your name]

SAMPLE LETTER: REQUEST FOR CREDIT REPORT (NO DENIAL)

[Your address]
[Date]

[Credit Bureau]
[Address]

To whom it may concern:

Enclosed is a check for $**[amount]** to cover the indicated cost of providing me with a copy of my credit report. Please send the credit report as soon as possible to the name and address below:

[Name]
[Present address]
[Previous address]
[Social Security number]
[Date of birth]

Thank you very much for your immediate attention.

Sincerely yours,
[Your signature]

[Your name]

Chapter 6

Credit scoring

Your credit history has been reduced to a three-digit number, and you should know what that number is, especially if you plan to purchase anything on credit soon. This three-digit number is most commonly known as a FICO score. (FICO is an acronym for Fair Isaac and Co., the company that began developing credit-scoring systems in the 1950s.) The people at FICO claim to use 30 different factors to determine risk. However, they won't disclose the exact formula for arriving at these scores. All three of the major credit bureaus (Equifax, Trans Union, and Experian) use FICO scores.

Credit scoring uses your credit history to evaluate the likelihood of your loan going into default. Scoring has been used in the credit card and installment loan industries for years. Now, credit scores are also being used in the mortgage industry. Having a credit score helps lenders streamline underwriting by quickly categorizing borrowers. A high credit score may mean that your application will receive only a superficial review by the prospective lender. A very low score, on the other hand, may get you a quick review and denial. In fact, if you do discover you have a low FICO, you're in excellent company. In 1997, Federal Reserve Governor Lawrence Lindsey was denied a Toys R Us credit card for a low FICO.

Your score will fall somewhere between 300 and 900; most consumers fall somewhere between 500 and 800. A FICO in the 500s is a very low score, which translates to lenders as high risk. The 600s is considered a medium score. Your payment history will be closely scrutinized and written explanations regarding the derogatory credit will likely be required prior to issuing any credit. Many lenders will not lend to someone with a FICO of less than 640. A FICO of 680 or higher is considered a high score, which means low risk for the lender and lower costs to the consumer. To assist you in understanding why a bureau returned a low FICO score, each reporting agency provides up to four reason codes when posting a FICO score on a credit report. These reason or adverse action codes are the primary factors contributing to the compilation of an individual's score. If these factors are addressed, the FICO score can usually be impacted in positive manner.

Here are a few of the factors affecting your FICO scores:

- ❑ Delinquencies.
- ❑ Too many accounts opened within the last twelve months.
- ❑ Short credit history.
- ❑ Balances on revolving credit are near the maximum limits.
- ❑ Public records, such as tax liens, judgments, or bankruptcies.
- ❑ No recent credit card balances.
- ❑ Too many recent credit inquiries.
- ❑ Too few revolving accounts.
- ❑ Too many revolving accounts.

FICO scores are only "guidelines" and factors other than FICO scores affect underwriting decisions. Here are some examples of compensating factors that will make a prospective lender more lenient toward lower FICO scores:

- ❑ A larger down payment.
- ❑ Low debt-to-income ratios.
- ❑ An excellent history of saving money.
- ❑ Previous paid loan with current lender.
- ❑ Availability of home equity or other collateral.

There also may be a reasonable explanation for items on the credit history that negatively impact your credit score.

Even so, credit scores may often not seem to make any sense at all. One borrower with a completely spotless credit history had a FICO score below 600. Another borrower with a foreclosure on her credit report had a FICO above 780.

What can I do about my credit score?

Credit scores are based on many different factors, which the credit agencies are forever tweaking and adjusting as new data is gathered. It is very difficult to identify any specific thing you can do to improve a credit score, but here are some ideas:

Do not apply for credit with a lot of different lenders or for new credit cards in the months before you apply for a loan. The number of credit inquiries is a factor in your score. An unusually large number of inquiries can lower your score.

Reduce your credit card balances to less than half your approved credit limits. It is not necessary to pay off your credit cards, but pushing the credit limit will reduce your score.

You can repair your credit using some of the techniques in this book.

Can I "fix" my credit?

You may want to begin your research by ordering a credit report from the three major credit bureaus listed in Chapter 5. This way, if there are any errors on your report, you can get them corrected. Credit bureaus are required to respond to your written request within 30 days. It is important that you know that even cleaning up any discrepancies with the credit bureaus will not immediately raise your score. It may take 60 to 90 days for either derogatory or positive marks to significantly impact a FICO.

In conclusion, here is a word of advice not directly related to FICO scores. When people begin to think about the possibility of buying a home, they often think about buying other big-ticket items, such as cars. Quite often, when someone asks a lender to pre-qualify them for a home loan, there is a brand new car payment on the credit report. In some cases, they would have qualified in their anticipated price range except that the new car payment has raised their debt-to-income ratio, thus lowering their maximum available purchase price. Sometimes the car was purchased so recently that the new loan doesn't even show up on the credit report yet. But with six to eight credit inquiries from car dealers and automobile finance companies, it is kind of obvious. Every time you sit down in a car dealership, it can end up generating several inquiries into your credit. Nowadays, good credit scores are essential if you want to get the best interest rate available. Guard your FICO score like a valuable possession. Don't open new revolving accounts needlessly. Don't fill out credit applications needlessly. Do not keep your credit cards nearly maxed out. Make sure you do use your credit occasionally, however, in order to show a prompt repayment history. Always make sure every creditor has its payment in its office no later than 29 days past due. And never, ever be more than 30 days late on your mortgage.

Chapter 7

Special problems facing previously married people

An increasing number of households are now headed by previously married people. This chapter deals with various credit situations that individuals may encounter when they divorce, separate, or become widowed. Unlike the other chapters in this book, the problems presented here do not focus on any particular federal law. In some instances, credit problems that arise with individuals who were previously married may have to be settled in court. Remember that situations will vary among individuals and among states. Therefore, the answers presented here are general in nature and may not apply to all cases. They should be considered only as a guide to credit problems for previously married individuals.

Q: My husband recently died, and now I find that the credit accounts that were in his name only have been cut off. Can creditors do this even if I have a substantial income from my husband's estate?

A: Yes. If your husband's credit accounts were in his name only, creditors may discontinue your use of them upon his death. You may, however, reapply for credit in your own name.

Q: My wife ran up sizable bills on my credit card at department stores before we were separated. Am I responsible for paying her bills?

A: Yes. If the credit accounts are in your name, you are responsible for the bills. You should, however, notify the creditors, preferably in writing, that your wife is no longer authorized to charge on your accounts. She would then have to open accounts in her name and be considered for credit on her own.

In many states, however, there is an old legal doctrine called "the law of necessaries" that makes a person responsible for certain debts incurred by the spouse, such as bills for food, clothing, and shelter. In some states, obligations under the doctrine cease upon separation, but in other states a spouse can be held liable for necessaries until a divorce decree is entered.

The bills in question would have to be settled between you and your wife should you seek a divorce or some separation that involves a settlement.

Q: My husband left, and now I am receiving calls from creditors for items that he purchased for his own use. Am I responsible for his bills?

A: If the accounts were in both names, you are also responsible for the bills. If the accounts were in his name only, you are not responsible. Should you and your husband separate or divorce, the matter of these debts should be part of your legal settlement.

Q: My spouse and I recently separated. Can I prevent my spouse from using our joint credit cards?

A: If either party of a joint account notifies the creditor that he or she wants to close the account, the creditor will close it. Neither party will then be able to use it. Both spouses can then apply for credit in their own names based upon their creditworthiness. Since the account was a joint account, both spouses are liable for all charges made up to the time the account was closed.

Q: I am separated from my husband and receive monthly child-support payments from him. Must I disclose these payments when I apply for credit in my own name?

A: No, you don't have to disclose monthly child-support payments. If you decide to disclose them, a creditor who considers income as part of a credit application must consider child-support payments as part of your income if they are made on a regular basis.

Q: Must credit bureaus maintain separate files on me now that I am divorced from my spouse?

A: Yes, credit bureaus must report information about you separately. However, that information may include your credit history on accounts that you held jointly with your spouse prior to your divorce, or information on accounts that were in your spouse's name but authorized for your use.

Q: My former spouse was a poor credit risk and had an unfavorable credit history. Can I be denied credit after we divorce based on information creditors receive about accounts I shared with my ex-spouse?

A: According to the Equal Credit Opportunity Act (ECOA), if you have been denied credit simply because an ex-spouse was a poor credit risk, a creditor must consider any information that you can offer to show that the unfavorable credit history on a former joint account does not accurately reflect your own credit history. In addition, the Fair Credit Reporting Act allows you to include a statement of dispute concerning inaccurate information on your credit report.

Q: After our divorce, my ex-spouse declared bankruptcy. Will that affect my credit rating?

A: Not if the bankruptcy occurred after your divorce. Once you are divorced, the credit history of your ex-spouse would have no effect on your credit standing. The ECOA requires creditors to consider applicants on the basis of their own creditworthiness and not that of their spouses or ex-spouses.

Chapter 8

Women, minorities, and credit

The Equal Credit Opportunity Act (ECOA) was enacted by Congress to eliminate discrimination against women seeking to obtain credit. It was expanded to include the prohibition of denying credit based on a person's race, color, place of national origin, religion, sex, age, or marital status. Further, a woman who exercises her rights under the act cannot be "blacklisted" from obtaining credit.

One of the main problems with the ECOA is that it is difficult to prove discrimination since other reasons can be given for denial of credit. Another problem is that the people the law was designed to protect seldom exercise their rights, usually because of one of the following reasons:

- ❑ Because credit rejection may be masqueraded by another reason, the applicant may not even realize she has been a victim of discrimination.
- ❑ Most people don't know their rights under the law and are unaware of the ease of filing a complaint.
- ❑ The applicant may not want to get involved with "fighting the system."

The general rule of thumb to determine whether you have been a victim of discrimination is to ask yourself if you would have been granted the loan if you were a non-minority with the same economic status. The following is a summary of your rights under the ECOA:

- ❑ If you have a sufficient debt-to-income ratio, the lender cannot require a cosigner or co-applicant.
- ❑ If you are a woman, you may use your maiden or married name (whichever you choose). You may even use a combination of both.
- ❑ The creditor may inquire as to how many dependents you have to determine your spendable income. However, he cannot ask about your birth-control practices or plans for parenthood.
- ❑ The creditor must consider all income derived from alimony, child support, public assistance, and part-time work. (A woman may choose not to reveal alimony and child support. If she chooses not to, these amounts will not be taken into consideration when computing her debt-to-income ratio.)
- ❑ A woman cannot be denied credit automatically for listing her occupation as a housewife.
- ❑ If there is a change in a woman's marital status (divorced, widowed, separated) or she chooses to change her name legally, the creditor cannot automatically require her to reapply for an existing loan. The only exception is if there appears to be a problem with a loan in which a former husband's income had been considered at the time the loan was approved.
- ❑ A woman's marital status cannot be inquired into if she is trying to obtain separate unsecured credit. The only exception is if the applicant lives in a community property state (Arizona, California, Idaho, Louisiana, Nevada, New Mexico, Texas, or Washington).

Equal Credit Opportunity Act

COMPLAINT LETTER

[Your address]

[Date]

Federal Trade Commission

[Address]

Re: **[Name and address of bank and your account number]**

To whom it may concern:

Please accept this letter as a formal complaint about the above-referenced bank. My complaint is as follows:

[Detail the specific violations committed by the bank.]

I have attempted to resolve this issue directly with **[name of bank]** to no avail. The key person I dealt with was **[name and title of contact person]**. Enclosed are photocopies of all related paperwork to document my claim.

Thank you for your attention to this matter.

Sincerely yours,

[Your signature]

[Your name]

Chapter 9

Disputing with the credit bureaus

The federal government enacted the Fair Credit Reporting Act on April 25, 1971, to protect consumers against the reporting of inaccurate, misleading, or obsolete information. Lawmakers designed the law to ensure that consumer-reporting agencies operate in a responsible and equitable manner. Appendix A includes a complete version of the Fair Credit Reporting Act, including amendments set forth in the Consumer Credit Reporting Reform Act of 1996.

The Fair Credit Reporting Act (FCRA)

The FCRA provides a list of rights and procedures that will assist you in clearing away negative remarks and reestablishing your creditworthiness—regardless of your previous credit history. By understanding your rights and using the law to your advantage, it's possible to remove bankruptcy, judgments, late payments, collection accounts, charge-offs, and other negative information from your files permanently.

The first step is to obtain copies of your credit reports from each of the major credit bureaus. You can find the address of your local credit bureau in the yellow pages under "Credit-Reporting Agencies." If you have been denied credit within the past 60 days, you can obtain a free copy of your report by enclosing a photocopy of the denial letter along with your request. Be sure to include your full name, date of birth, Social Security number, and addresses for the past five years. If you have not been denied credit within the last 60 days, you may purchase a copy of your report from each credit bureau. In California, for example, the cost for a copy of your report is $8 from each of the major bureaus. The cost may vary in other states.

You also have the right to visit the credit bureau in person to review your file. Simply call the bureau and make an appointment. You will then need to present the proper identification and pay the required fee. The law also allows you to be accompanied by one other person of your choosing.

If you request your credit report by mail, you should receive a copy within three weeks. You will also receive an explanation of the various codes and abbreviations the report contains.

According to the FCRA, you have the right to dispute any remark on your report that you "reasonably believe" to be inaccurate or incomplete. The act requires the credit bureau to reinvestigate those disputed items within "a reasonable period of time"—interpreted by the Federal Trade Commission as 30 days. If the bureau finds that the information was incorrect, obsolete, or could no longer be verified, it must correct or delete the information.

If the bureau does not respond to your initial dispute within a "reasonable time," follow up with another letter. This time, demand that the bureau respond to your dispute immediately to prevent your being forced to take legal action. Give them about two weeks to comply and be sure to maintain copies of all correspondence.

If the bureau persists in violating your rights by refusing to reinvestigate your legitimate dispute, send them a final letter demanding action. This time, send copies of your letter, along with the original request, to the Federal Trade Commission and your local office of the attorney general.

How to dispute

1. Obtain a credit report and analyze the report for items you believe to be inaccurate, incorrect, or obsolete. For example, you thought you owed $800 on your Visa card account. The account is presently under collection, but your Experian credit report shows a balance of $900. This is inaccurate, and you have a right to dispute the entire account.
2. Send the bureau a dispute form (enclosed with your credit report). If you don't have a consumer dispute form, you may copy the one at the end of this chapter or use a blank piece of paper. Question only two or three items at a time so that your dispute will not appear to be frivolous.

   On the dispute form, be sure to include the items you are disputing, the names of the creditors (subscribers), and the relevant account numbers. Indicate why you believe that item is being reported incorrectly (such as the amount owed is incorrect, the account is not yours, the account has been paid in full, the number of late payments is incorrect, etc.).
3. If you do not receive a response within six weeks of sending your dispute form, immediately send a follow-up letter (see sample on page 86).
4. Obtain results of the credit bureau's reinvestigation. Most credit bureaus will notify you of the result of the investigation and send you a copy of your updated credit report.
5. Wait at least six weeks.
6. Repeat the cycle from step one for another two to three items.
7. Keep a record of all correspondence. Make copies of all credit reports, disputes, replies, and responses. If the reply is by telephone, note the date and time of call,

the name of the person who called, and the nature of the conversation.

Summary of the dispute cycle

1. Obtain credit report.
2. Send dispute form.
3. Credit bureau verifies.
4. Disputed information checked with creditors.
5. Creditors respond to credit bureau investigation.
   A. Unverifiable information deleted.
   B. Incorrect information corrected.
   C. Correct information remains.

Consumer statements

Under the Fair Credit Reporting Act you have the right to add to your credit report a statement of up to 100 words regarding any item(s) you wish to clarify. This statement will then appear on all subsequent reports sent to your credit grantors.

The consumer statement has often proven to be a very effective tool. It is especially useful when the amount of the particular negative account is relatively small or you have plenty of positive items to cover the single negative item.

Here are some examples of consumer statements you can use:

- ❑ "Attention: Apparently someone has been using my identification to obtain credit. Please verify with me at [**phone number**] prior to extension of new credit."
- ❑ "Experian, a business for profit, violates my Constitutional right to privacy by maintaining my name in its computer bank against my wishes, places me in a false light while doing so, and appropriates my name for its commercial advantage. Experian has continually and persistently violated the California Consumer Credit Agencies Act and the federal Fair Credit Reporting Act

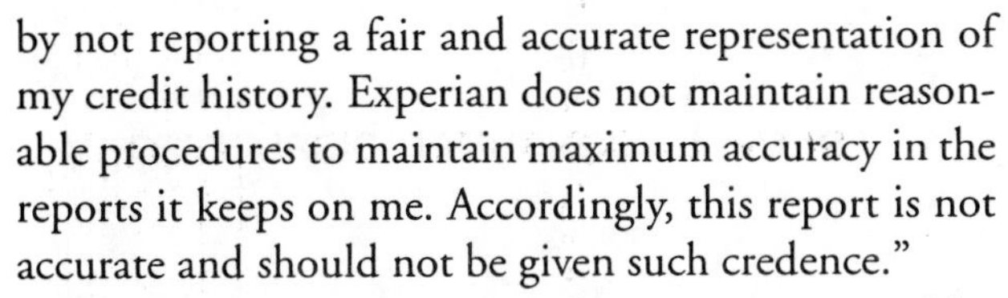

by not reporting a fair and accurate representation of my credit history. Experian does not maintain reasonable procedures to maintain maximum accuracy in the reports it keeps on me. Accordingly, this report is not accurate and should not be given such credence."

- ❑ "Attention: Due to the identification system used by Experian, it is apparent that my credit file has been merged with the file of someone else bearing the same name. Please contact either Trans Union or Equifax for an accurate report."
- ❑ "Attention: This is not my account. I have never owed money to this creditor. Apparently, a mistake was made in the reporting."
- ❑ "During the period from [**date**] to [**date**], I was laid off work without advance notice. I have always paid my creditors promptly and satisfactorily before and since that period. I have been gainfully employed with the same employer for [**length of employment**]."
- ❑ "On [**date**], I moved to another address. I notified all creditors, including [**name of creditor**] promptly. [**Creditor**] was slow in changing my address in its file. Subsequently, I did not receive my billing statement for [**length of time**]. Once I received the statement at my new address, I paid this creditor."

Be honest yet creative in writing your consumer statement. It could be extremely effective.

SAMPLE: CONSUMER DISPUTE FORM

Personal Identification *(Please print or type)*

Name ______________________________

(Last)(First)(M. Initial)(Suffix: Jr., Sr.)

Present address ______________________

(Street)

____

(City, State ZIP)

Former address ______________________

(Street)

____

(City, state ZIP)

Date of birth ______ **Social Security #** ___________

(M/D/Y)

I recently received a copy of the report confirming my credit history, and I disagree with the following information:

Credit History
[For each piece of information you disagree with, provide the name of the business, your account number, and the specifc nature of the disagreement.]

(cont'd.)

(cont'd)

Public record and other information

[For each piece of information in this category, provide the court or business, the case number or your account number, and the specific nature of the disagreement.]

Other

[List any other information you disagree with here, such as information from other credit bureaus. Include the item and the specific nature of the disagreement.]

I understand that the information I have disputed will be rechecked when necessary at the source, and I will be notified of the results of this recheck.

________________________ ___________

(Signature) (Date)

SAMPLE LETTER: FOLLOW-UP TO A DISPUTE

[Your address]

[Date]

[Name of credit bureau]

Consumer Relations Department

[Address]

To whom it may concern:

On **[date you originated the dispute]**, I sent you a request to investigate certain items on my credit report that I believe to be incorrect or inaccurate. But as of today, six weeks have passed, and I have not yet received a response from you. Under the Fair Credit Reporting Act, you are required to respond within "a reasonable time." If the information cannot be verified, please delete it from my credit report. I would appreciate your immediate attention to this matter and your informing me of the result.

Yours sincerely,

[Your signature]

[Your name]

[Address]

[Social Security number]

[Date of birth]

SAMPLE LETTER: SECOND FOLLOW-UP LETTER

[Your address]
[Date]

[Name of credit bureau]
Consumer Relations Department
[Address]

RE: **[Your name and Social Security number]**

To whom it may concern:

Four weeks ago, I sent you a letter stating that you had neither responded to nor investigated my disputes of incorrect items found on my credit report. Copies of that letter and the original dispute letter are enclosed. To date, you still have not complied with your obligation under the Fair Credit Reporting Act.

If I do not receive your response within the next two weeks, I will file a complaint with the Federal Trade Commission. In addition, I will not hesitate to retain my attorney to pursue my right to recover damages under the Fair Credit Reporting Act.

Please also forward me the names and addresses of individuals you contacted to verify the information so I may follow up. Thank you for your immediate attention.

Sincerely yours,

[Your signature]

[Your name]

Chapter 10

Disputing with creditors directly

This method works very much like the one discussed in the previous chapter. In this case, however, the dispute letters are directed to the creditors themselves (such as department stores, collection agencies, banks, etc.) rather than the credit bureaus.

As subscribers, creditors have direct access to your credit bureau files. They also have the authority to change or delete information from your credit report.

This method is initiated by sending the creditor a formal letter identifying the account you are disputing, stating the reason for your dispute, and demanding that it correct or delete the negative item. You should also inform the creditor that if the matter is not resolved quickly, you will take legal action (see Chapter 12).

Collection agencies will sometimes refuse to change your credit rating unless specifically instructed by the creditor that assigned them the account. In one case, a credit consultant was negotiating a settlement with a collection agency on behalf of a client. The collection agency had a reputation for being a tough negotiator. After two weeks, the negotiations broke down. The consultant went directly to the bank that had assigned the account to the agency. The consultant reached a settlement with the bank, which instructed the agency to remove the account from the client's credit report.

When disputing with a creditor, there are several important points to remember:

- ❑ You must let the creditor know that it was the one at fault. For example, it provided you with substandard service, its merchandise was defective, it misplaced your check, it did not deliver the goods, or it somehow did not perform its part of the agreement.
- ❑ Even if you were at fault, you can still get positive results. For example, one woman discovered a "30-day late payment" on her credit report. The account was from a major department store with which she had maintained an account for more than 12 years. She was at fault for making that late payment. However, she approached the credit manager and asked him to remove the negative remark from her report, indicating that she had always been a good customer. The credit manager complied with her request for public-relations purposes.
- ❑ You may need to send this dispute letter all the way up to the chairman of the board to get a response.

SAMPLE LETTER: DISPUTE WITH CREDITOR

[Your address]
[Date]

[Name of creditor]
[Address]

Re: **[Account number]**

To whom it may concern:

I have recently obtained a credit report from [**credit bureau**]. It shows that the above account with your company was **[reason for dispute]**. According to my recollection, I have always paid this account promptly and satisfactorily. This incorrect information is injurious to my credit rating. I would appreciate it if you would verify this information and correct it with the above-named credit bureau immediately. If the information cannot be verified, please delete the account from my credit report.

Your immediate attention to this matter will be greatly appreciated.

Sincerely yours,
[Your signature]

[Your name]

Chapter 11

Negotiation strategies

Aaron purchased a new stereo system for $975. Three months later, he was laid off from his job. His income went from $35,000 a year to unemployment benefits of $3,600 over six months and then ran out entirely. He was a responsible person, but there was no way he could maintain the stereo payments during this crisis. Aaron finally got another job. When he explained his situation and that he wanted desperately to remove the negative mark on his credit record, the company's credit manager agreed to settle the debt for $525. Aaron took the letter he got in exchange and sent it to the local credit bureau. The bureau reinvestigated the item and marked it as paid in full.

This technique is often successful with managers of finance companies. Because of the high turnover, they are usually eager to establish a record of having collected money on accounts that were already written off. Remember that you have the bargaining power at this point. The money you are now offering is money the creditor never expected to receive. Since it is like new money coming in, he will usually be willing to negotiate.

This the most effective and ethical method of credit restoration, and it is a win-win situation. The creditor gets paid, and you get the negative information removed from your credit report.

Steps of the negotiation cycle

1. Contact the creditor by phone and reach a tentative agreement.
2. Send the creditor a settlement agreement, requesting return of a signed copy.
3. Upon receipt of a signed copy, send a money order marked "Full Payment."
4. Order a credit report from the credit bureau to ensure the item is changed or deleted as agreed.
5. If your credit report is unchanged, send the creditor a letter demanding compliance with the agreement.

Agreeing on a repayment rate

Your bargaining power in this technique is your willingness to repay your creditor the money that you owe him. If the account has already been charged off or discharged in bankruptcy, your leverage will be even greater. At this point, the creditor has already accepted a loss on your account, and he does not expect to ever see or hear from you again. When he hears that you are now willing to repay the debt (or even a percentage of the debt), he'll be anxious to work with you.

You should expect to repay your creditor from 70 percent to the full amount to have it removed or to change the negative credit rating. However, if you expect to settle at 70 percent or less, you should start by offering around 40 percent. You will also lose some of your bargaining power if the balance on the account is under $200, as the creditor may not even want to waste his time with it.

In many cases, the initial person with whom you begin negotiating does not have the authority to enter into a settlement agreement, especially since it involves changing your credit rating. It is important, therefore, that you talk directly to someone who is in a position to authorize the final agreement.

Getting information changed in or deleted from your file

Another obstacle you may face is that many of these collection officers will tell you that it is impossible (or illegal) to change your credit rating. Therefore, it is often necessary for you to explain to them what you want and how it can be done. The creditor can use the following methods to change or delete credit information on your file:

- ❑ All creditors who subscribe to one of the major credit bureaus use a nine-track computerized magnetic tape to report their clients' payment histories. They send this tape to the bureau on a monthly basis. Therefore, you can request that they change the information on this tape after they receive your payment. You may also ask them to delete the account from the tape.
- ❑ The creditor can also "bull's-eye" your account. This is an instant method of credit file correction, which is accomplished through the creditor's computer link to the credit bureau. The creditor has the capacity to pull up your account on the computer and make the necessary change automatically. By using a change of information slip, the authorized person can send the corrected information to the data acquisition department of the credit bureau and your file will be updated.
- ❑ The creditor can also change the information by submitting a manual update form to the consumer relations department of the credit bureau. With this method, the creditor can delete negative information but cannot change the rating from negative to positive.

When negotiating with the creditor, it is essential that you know exactly what you are trying to accomplish. Your priority is to have the account deleted or removed completely from your credit report. This is especially true when you are negotiating with a collection agency that has reported your account to the credit bureau. You definitely do not want the name of any collection agency appearing on your credit report. Its name alone is considered a negative item by most credit grantors.

Positive, nonrated, or negative rating of your file

If the creditor will not delete the account from your report completely, the next best thing would be to have the negative remark changed to a positive remark. For example:

- ❑ Paid Satisfactory/Paid as Agreed.
- ❑ Current Account/No Late Payments.
- ❑ Credit Line Closed/Consumer's Request.

The lowest rating you will accept in your negotiation should be "nonrated account." For example:

- ❑ Paid.
- ❑ Settled as a Nonrated Account.

Under no circumstances should you accept a negative rating, such as:

- ❑ Paid Collection.
- ❑ Paid Charge-Off.
- ❑ Paid, Was 30 (or 60, 90, 120) Days Late.

If the creditor will not delete the account or change the rating to a positive remark, then you should turn to other methods of credit restoration for that specific account.

Successful negotiation takes patience and persistence. Do not show the creditor that you are too anxious to settle. After you have made your offer, wait for the creditor to accept it or make a counteroffer. Always make it clear when you begin negotiating that your only incentive to settle is to restore your credit rating. Therefore, a positive correction or deletion of the account is essential to any agreement. If a creditor is interested in settling, it knows that you will settle only if a better credit rating is part of the deal.

After reaching an agreement on the phone but before making any payment, confirm the agreement in writing by sending the creditor a settlement agreement like the one included at the end of this chapter. Have the creditor sign the agreement and return a copy to you before you send the money. This is essential because there have been many cases where a collection agency agreed to everything on the telephone but, after receiving the money, denied any promises had been made and refused to follow through on its end of the bargain. With a signed agreement clearly stating the responsibility of each party, both should honor their part of the contract. Otherwise, the creditor could face legal action for breach of contract as well as fraud.

Other considerations

Timing is essential in negotiating a good settlement agreement. A bank is a highly departmentalized institution. When your loan is still in the current-loan servicing department, the bank has no incentive to settle with you or change your credit rating. It expects you to pay what you owe as agreed. Successful negotiating can start when the loan is in the collection department, charge-off department, or legal department. At this point, the bank has given up hope on you and should be glad to settle the account.

If you are facing a temporary cash-flow problem, you can try this to lower your monthly payments and avoid filing bankruptcy: Explain your financial problem to your creditors and offer to make monthly payments of four percent of the balance of the accounts. This is a reasonable offer and should be acceptable to many creditors as an alternative to bankruptcy. You can always increase your monthly payments later, when you are in a better financial position.

You may also want to consider the services of Consumer Credit Counselors, a nonprofit organization that will negotiate on your behalf for a nominal fee. You can find the address in your local telephone directory. Many lenders are willing to work with this organization because of its national reputation.

The conditional endorsement

This is an extremely powerful and little-known method for reducing outstanding debts and restoring your credit rating. It is known as the "conditional endorsement" technique.

You begin by getting the creditor to agree to the amount of the debt settlement, but without requesting the creditor to change your credit rating (not yet, anyway). Once the creditor has agreed to accept your final payment, you can send them a check stapled to the following memorandum of agreement: "I accept this payment on [**account #**] as payment in full. I agree that this account will be reported to all credit bureaus as 'paid satisfactorily.' I further agree to deem any additional amount as uncollectable." This same information must also be typed in the "endorsement" section on the back of your check. Then on the front of the check, in the memo section, you write "payment in full on [**account #**]." The combination of this information written on both sides of your check along with a separate document stapled to the check comprises a complete legal document. By endorsing the check, the creditor has entered into a legal contract to perform the conditions of the agreement. If they do not follow up with their end of the agreement, they can be taken to court and they will owe you money for breach of contract.

SAMPLE LETTER: SETTLEMENT AGREEMENT

[Your address]
[Date]

[Name of creditor]
Attn: **[Contact person]**
[Address]

RE: **[Account number]**

Dear **[Contact person]**:

To confirm our telephone conversation on **[date]** regarding the above account: I will pay your company $**[amount]** as full settlement of this account. Your company has agreed to change the remark on my credit file to "Paid Satisfactorily." In addition, any references to late payment or charge-off regarding this account will be deleted from my credit file.

If this is acceptable to your company, please sign in the space provided below and return a copy to me. Upon receipt of this signed acknowledgment, I will forward you a cashier's check in the amount stated above.

Thank you for your immediate attention.

____

(Signature of authorized officer)

Date __________

Yours sincerely,

[Your name]

Chapter 12
Aggressive legal tactics

If previous methods have been unsuccessful, or if a particular creditor or credit bureau persists in violating your legal rights, you may also use the court system to help restore your credit.

Your rights under the Fair Credit Reporting Act

If a credit bureau refuses to investigate a legitimate dispute by claiming it is "frivolous and irrelevant," you can obtain an attorney and file a lawsuit against the bureau for noncompliance with the Fair Credit Reporting Act or similar state statutes. While the trial is pending, your attorney can file a motion for injunctive relief. Because the negative remarks on your credit report may threaten basic living—such as renting an apartment, obtaining employment, writing a check, obtaining loans for your business, etc.—the court may grant this motion.

In many cases, the matter may not be adjudicated for several years. In the meantime, your attorney can ask the court to order the credit bureau to refrain temporarily from including any negative items under dispute in your credit file until the case is resolved. If the court rules the motion in your favor, the credit bureau will be compelled by law to refrain from reporting the disputed negative information.

Another method is to file a complaint against the credit bureau in small-claims court. Terms vary among states, but in California, the filing fee is only $20, and a claimant can recover up to $5,000 in damages. Such damages may include denial of credit, stress, humiliation, or punitive damages for willful noncompliance with state and federal laws. If enough consumers followed this route, it would create an incentive for the credit bureaus to start obeying the law and fulfilling their responsibilities under the Fair Credit Reporting Act.

If you intend to file a lawsuit against a credit bureau, it is essential that you keep accurate records of all correspondence. The key to using the courts successfully is sufficient evidence. Be sure to maintain copies of credit reports, loan denials, and all other documentation relating to your case.

If enough people got together, it would also be possible to file a class-action suit against a credit bureau that persists in violating the rights of consumers. This would begin with a group of individuals who have received letters from a certain credit bureau refusing to investigate their disputes. Filing a class-action suit against a major credit bureau could possibly make a serious dent in the bureaucratic machinery. Class-action suits have often resulted in awards of several million dollars.

The following is a summary of your legal rights under the Fair Credit Reporting Act:

- ❑ To be told the nature and source of the information collected about you by a credit bureau.
- ❑ To obtain this information free of charge when you have been denied credit, insurance, or employment within 60 days. Otherwise, the reporting agency can charge a reasonable fee for the disclosure.
- ❑ To take any one person of your choosing with you when you visit the credit bureau.
- ❑ To be told who has received your credit report within the preceding six months, or within the preceding two years if it was furnished for employment purposes.

- ❑ To have incomplete, incorrect, or obsolete information reinvestigated and, if found to be inaccurate or unverifiable, to have such information removed from your file.
- ❑ When a dispute between you and the credit bureau cannot be resolved, to have your version of the dispute placed in the file and included in future reports.
- ❑ To request the credit bureau to send your consumer statement to all future credit grantors.
- ❑ To have a credit report withheld from anyone who does not have a legitimate business need for the information it contains.
- ❑ To sue a company for damages if it willingly or negligently violates the law and, if the suit is successful, to collect attorney's fees and court costs.
- ❑ To be notified if a company is requesting an investigative consumer report.
- ❑ To request from a company that ordered an investigative report further information as to the nature and scope of the investigation.
- ❑ To have negative information removed from your report after seven years. One major exception is bankruptcy, which may be reported for 10 years.

Letter from the Federal Trade Commission

UNITED STATES OF AMERICA
FEDERAL TRADE COMMISSION

Mr. Robert Hammond

Re: Correspondence No. 1684890011988

Dear Mr. Hammond:

Thank you for your letter concerning a problem with your credit report and a credit bureau that is reporting information about you.

Enclosed for your information is a brochure describing the Fair Credit Reporting Act (FCRA) that you may find helpful.

You have the right under the FCRA to be told what information is in your file at the credit bureau and the source of the information. You can ask the credit bureau for this disclosure either in person, or by telephone if you have first sent a written request that properly identifies yourself (usually your name, current address, and Social Security number). Some credit bureaus will mail you a copy of your file, but they are not required to do so.

If you believe an item in your credit report is inaccurate or is not complete, the FCRA gives you the right to dispute this information. You should write the credit bureau and tell it that a dispute exists regarding a particular item of information. It is often useful to provide the credit bureau with any information that you might have that would assist its investigation efforts. We suggest that you send your dispute via certified mail, and that you retain a copy for your records.

Credit bureaus are required to investigate your dispute within a reasonable period of time, generally 30 days, unless the bureau has reasonable grounds to believe the dispute is frivolous or irrelevant. If the item is wrong or can no longer be checked, it must be dropped from your file. If, after the credit bureau has concluded its investigation, you still don't agree that your report is accurate, you should write a short statement of 100 words or less giving your side of the situation. This statement then becomes part of your credit report. At your request, the credit bureau must report the change to anyone who received a copy of your report during the past six months.

Once a credit bureau has verified an item of information, it is entitled to continue to report that piece of information on your credit report.

If you still dispute the accuracy of the information being reported, we suggest that you contact the responsible creditor directly and attempt to resolve the problem at its source. Negative credit information generally may be reported for seven years with the exception of a bankruptcy, which may be reported for 10 years.

One important point to keep in mind is that even though you paid off a credit account that was previously delinquent, the credit bureau can still report the fact that you were behind in your payments when you finally paid off the account. A credit report showing that you paid off a debt after it became delinquent is usually considered to be adverse information by creditors, but not as adverse as a credit report showing that you haven't paid off the debt.

If you feel that your credit report does not accurately portray your creditworthiness, Regulation B—which implements the Equal Opportunity Act—provides that you have the right to present information to your prospective creditor to show that your credit report does not reflect your ability or willingness to repay. The creditor must consider this information at your request. If you know there is adverse information on your credit report, it is often best to explain the circumstances surrounding the item and to provide other positive information to the creditor.

We cannot act as your lawyer or intervene in a dispute between a consumer and a credit bureau or a reporter of information. The FCRA does give you the right to bring suit on your own behalf for willful and negligent violations of the Act. You may also be able to recover attorney's fees. If you believe the FCRA has been violated, we suggest that you consult a private attorney or your local legal services organization.

Thank you for bringing your experience to our attention.

Sincerely,

Los Angeles Regional Office

11000 Wilshire Blvd.

Federal Building

Los Angeles, CA 90024

Document(s) 5873

Chapter 13

Questions and answers about credit repair

Q: Is it really possible to "erase" bad credit?

A: Yes. By following the various procedures outlined in this book it is possible to remove all types of negative information from your credit files. For example, a credit bureau is required by law to reinvestigate disputed information with the creditor (subscriber). If the information is found to be inaccurate, it must be corrected. If the information is obsolete, it must be deleted. If the information can no longer be verified, it must be deleted. Also, by negotiating directly with the creditor, it is possible to have the creditor instruct the bureau to remove or correct the bad credit information in your file.

Q: What can I do with accounts that I have paid already but that show up with a negative remark?

A: Many creditors have already closed your file after you paid them off and stored the closed file at another location. They do not have the time to dig out those records and verify the information whenever someone disputes an old account. Therefore, the information may not be verified when the credit bureau reinvestigates the dispute. If the information is not verified, it must be deleted from your credit report.

Q: How do I improve my credit report after filing bankruptcy?

A: The debts that were discharged during bankruptcy will show up on your credit report as either "Charge-off" or "Bk Liq Reo." The bankruptcy itself will appear under public record information as Chapter 7 or Chapter 13. The only way to remove the bankruptcy itself from your credit report is to dispute it directly with the credit bureaus. You can often find some mistake in the reporting of the information. Some people simply deny that they ever filed the bankruptcy, although this is definitely not recommended. Normally, the bankruptcy will remain on your credit report for up to 10 years unless it is removed through dispute.

As to the items that were charged off by your creditors when you filed bankruptcy, the most effective way to remove these items is through direct negotiation with the creditors. (See Chapter 10.) Negotiate with your creditors so that, in return for your repaying a portion of the debt, they agree to change your credit rating or delete the accounts from your credit reports.

Another alternative is to add a consumer statement to your credit report. This statement, which can be up to 100 words, allows you to tell your side of the story. In some cases, people have indicated in their consumer statements that they never filed for bankruptcy or that all the accounts included in the bankruptcy have since been paid in full.

Q: How can I remove a defaulted student loan from my credit report?

A: This will depend on who reported the account to the credit bureau. There are three possible entities: the Student Loan Commission (i.e., the government), the bank that financed the student loan, or the collection agency. If the Student Loan Commission reported the delinquent account, the only way you can remove it is to pay off the loan in full and then dispute it with the credit bureau. You can inform the bureau that the loan has now been paid in full (only if it has, of course). The credit bureau will then have to verify the information with the Student Loan Commission. Since the commission has to service so many loans, it is very possible that it may not verify with the credit bureau that your loan was ever in default. If the bank or the collection agency reported the delinquent student loan, then you can use the creditor negotiation strategy outlined in Chapter 11.

Q: What is a judgment and how can I remove it from my credit report?

A: A judgment is a court order to pay a certain obligation. The judgment becomes part of public record and will appear on all future credit reports. If a judgment has already been entered against you and has appeared on your credit report, there are several possible approaches you can take:

- ❑ If you haven't been served with the lawsuit, have your attorney file a motion to "vacate judgment" with the court. After the court grants you the motion (assuming the time to file such a motion has not run out), send a court-certified copy of the court decision to all the credit bureaus that have recorded your judgment and demand that they remove it immediately.
- ❑ If you have already received a judgment and you have been served, but perhaps improperly, you can still negotiate your way out of the judgment. The negotiation will involve two aspects:

  A. Call the creditor and claim that you have been served improperly with the lawsuit (you can only make this claim if you did not appear for the trial and a default judgment was entered against you), but you are willing to settle the case and pay them a portion of the claim. After you come to an agreement on the amount of settlement, you will have to stipulate to the fact that the creditor has served you improperly. Next, have your attorney file a motion to vacate judgment based on defective service, with the agreement by the creditor not to go to court to contest the motion. Before the motion is filed, however, the creditor must be paid the negotiated settlement amount.

B. Have your attorney file the motion to vacate judgment for you. Make sure, however, that you are within the time allowed by the statute of limitation to file such a motion before you begin. After the court grants the motion, have the court clerk certify several copies of the motion and mail a copy to each of the major credit bureaus, along with a cover letter stating that you want the judgment removed from your credit reports. This is a court order, and they will have to remove the judgment from your record immediately.

- ❑ Another alternative is to cover up your judgment with a good consumer statement. Before doing that, however, you have to satisfy the judgment and make sure the credit bureaus record the judgment as "satisfied" on your credit report. A good consumer statement should explain that you fought the lawsuit purposely for a legitimate reason, that the blame is really that of the creditor who sued you, and that you respect the court's final decision, having satisfied the judgment immediately.

Chapter 14

Starting over with a new credit file

If you have filed for bankruptcy, you may be the target of a credit-repair scheme called "file segregation." In this scheme, you are promised a chance to hide unfavorable credit information by establishing a new credit identity. That may sound perfect, especially if you're afraid that you won't get any credit as long as bankruptcy appears on your credit record. The problem is that file segregation is illegal. If you use it, you could face fines or even a prison sentence.

A new credit identity

If you have filed for bankruptcy, you may receive a letter from a credit-repair company that warns you about your inability to get credit cards, personal loans, or any other types of credit for 10 years. For a fee, the company promises to help you hide your bankruptcy and establish a new credit identity to use when you apply for credit. These companies also make pitches in classified ads, on the radio and TV, and even over the Internet.

If you pay the fee and sign up for their service, you may be directed to apply for an Employer Identification Number (EIN) from the Internal Revenue Service (IRS). Typically, EINs—which resemble Social Security numbers—are used by businesses to report financial information to the IRS and the Social Security Administration.

After you receive your EIN, the credit-repair service will tell you to use it in place of your Social Security number when you apply for credit. They'll also tell you to use a new mailing address and some credit references. (The credit references will come from new accounts, such as jewelry store credit cards, rent-to-own furniture accounts, etc., that you open with the new EIN and address.)

To convince you to establish a new credit identity, the credit-repair service is likely to make a variety of false claims. Listen carefully; these false claims, along with the pitch for getting a new credit identity, should alert you to the possibility of fraud. You'll probably hear:

Claim 1: You will not be able to get credit for 10 years (the period of time bankruptcy information may stay on your credit record). Each creditor has its own criteria for granting credit. While one may reject your application because of a bankruptcy, another may grant you credit shortly after you filed for bankruptcy. Given a new, reliable payment record, your chances of getting credit will probably increase as time passes.

Claim 2: The company or its file segregation program is affiliated with the federal government. The federal government does not support or work with companies that offer such programs.

Claim 3: The file segregation program is legal. It is a federal crime to make any false statements on a loan or credit application. The credit-repair company may advise you to do just that. It is a federal crime to misrepresent your Social Security number. It also is a federal crime to obtain an EIN from the IRS under false pretenses. Further, you could be charged with mail or wire fraud if you use the mail or the telephone to apply for credit and provide false information. Worse yet, file segregation would likely constitute civil fraud under many state laws.

The Credit Services Organization Act

This law prohibits false claims about credit repair and makes it illegal for these operations to charge you until they have performed their services. It requires these companies to tell you about your legal rights. Credit-repair companies must provide this in a written contract that also spells out just what services are to be performed, how long it will take to achieve results, the total cost, and any guarantees that are offered. Under the law, these contracts also must explain that consumers have three days to cancel at no charge.

You also have the right to sue in federal court. The law allows you to seek either your actual losses or the amount you paid the company, whichever is more. You also can seek punitive damages (sums of money to punish the company for violating the law). The law also allows class actions (cases where groups of consumers join together in one lawsuit) in federal court. If you win, the other side has to pay your attorney's fees.

Many states have laws regulating credit repair companies and may be helpful if you've lost money to credit repair scams.

If you've had a problem with a credit repair company, report the company. Contact your local consumer affairs office or your state attorney general (AG). Many AGs have toll-free consumer hotlines. Check with your local directory assistance.

You also may wish to contact the FTC. Although the Commission cannot resolve individual credit problems for consumers, it can act against a company if it sees a pattern of possible law violations. If you believe a company has engaged in credit fraud, you can send your complaint to: Consumer Response Center, Federal Trade Commission, Washington, DC 20580.

Identification theft

"I don't remember charging those items. I've never even been in that store."

Maybe you never charged those items, but someone else did—someone who used your name and personal information to commit fraud. When an imposter co-opts your name, your Social Security number, your credit card number, or some other piece of your personal information for his or her use—in short, when someone appropriates your personal information without your knowledge—it's a crime, pure and simple.

The biggest problem? You may not know your identity has been stolen until you discover that something's amiss. You may get bills for a credit card account you never opened, your credit report may include debts you never knew you had, a billing cycle may pass without your receiving a statement, or you may see charges on your bills that you didn't sign for, didn't authorize, and don't know anything about.

If someone has stolen your identity, the Federal Trade Commission recommends that you take three actions immediately.

First, **contact the fraud departments of each of the three major credit bureaus.** Tell them to flag your file with a fraud alert including a statement that creditors should call you for permission before they open any new accounts in your name.

Fraud departments of the major bureaus

Equifax (800) 522-6285

Experian (888) 397-3742

Trans Union (800) 680-7287

Second, **contact the creditors for any accounts that have been tampered with or opened fraudulently.** Speak with someone in the security or fraud department, and follow up in writing. Following up with a letter is one of the procedures spelled out in the Fair Credit Reporting Act for resolving errors on credit billing statements, including charges or electronic fund transfers that you have not made.

Third, **file a police report.** Keep a copy in case your creditors need proof of the crime.

Although identity thieves can wreak havoc on your personal finances, there are some things you can do to take control of the situation. Here's how to handle some of the most common forms of identity theft.

If an identity thief has stolen your mail for access to new credit cards, bank and credit card statements, pre-approved credit offers, and tax information, or falsified change-of-address forms, he or she has committed a crime. Report it to your local postal inspector. Also, always tear or shred your charge receipts, copies of credit applications, insurance forms, bank checks and statements, expired charge cards, and credit offers you get in the mail.

If you discover that an identity thief has changed the billing address on an existing credit card account, close the account. When you open a new account, ask that a password be used before any inquiries or changes can be made on the account. Avoid using easily available information such as your mother's maiden name, your birth date, the last four digits of your Social Security number, your phone number, or a series of consecutive numbers. Avoid the same information and numbers when you create a Personal Identification Number (PIN).

If you have reason to believe that an identity thief has accessed your bank accounts, checking account, or ATM card, close the accounts immediately. When you open new accounts, insist on password-only access. If your checks have been stolen or misused, stop payment. If your ATM card has been lost, stolen, or otherwise compromised, cancel the card and get another with a new PIN.

If an identity thief established new phone service in your name and is making long-distance calls, making unauthorized calls that appear to come from—and are billed to—your cellular phone, or using your calling card and PIN, contact your service provider immediately to cancel your account and calling card. Get new accounts and new PINs.

If it appears that someone is using your Social Security number when applying for a job, contact the Social Security Administration to verify the accuracy of your reported earnings and the correct reporting of your name. Call (800) 772-1213 to check your Personal Earnings and Benefit Estimate.

If you suspect that an identity thief is using your name or Social Security number to get a driver's license, contact your state's Department of Motor Vehicles. If your state uses your Social Security number as your driver's license number, ask to substitute another number.

For more information about identity theft, check out the federal government's central Web site on identity theft at www.consumer.gov/idtheft. You also may want to contact:

- ❑ The Privacy Rights Clearinghouse, which provides information on how to network with other identity theft victims. Call (619) 298-3396.
- ❑ The U.S. Secret Service, which has jurisdiction over financial fraud cases. Although the Service generally investigates cases where the dollar loss is substantial, your information may provide evidence of a larger pattern of fraud requiring their involvement. Contact your local field office.
- ❑ The Social Security Administration, which may issue you a new Social Security number if you still have difficulties even after trying to resolve the problems resulting from identity theft. Unfortunately, there is no guarantee that a new Social Security number will resolve your problems.
- ❑ The Federal Trade Commission is the federal clearinghouse for consumer complaints about identity theft. The information you provide can help the Commission and other law enforcement agencies track, investigate, and prosecute identity thieves.

The following press release was issued by the Federal Trade Commission:

Embargoed for 11:00 AM Release
For Release: February 2, 1999

Crackdown Hits 43 Phony Credit Firms That Turn Consumers into Felons

In a massive crackdown on operators who turn credit-challenged consumers into lawbreakers, the Federal Trade Commission (FTC) and National Association of Attorneys General (NAAG) announced today that 17 law enforcement agencies have filed 43 law enforcement actions against defendants who claim to help consumers obtain new credit histories through new identification numbers—a practice commonly known as "file segregation."

Using the Internet and other media to make claims such as "brand new credit file in 30 days," the suspect firms sell instructions about how consumers can substitute federally-issued, nine-digit employee identification numbers or taxpayer identification numbers for Social Security numbers and use them illegally to build new credit profiles that will allow them to get credit they may be denied based on their real credit histories. The FTC and NAAG cautioned that using a false identification number to apply for credit is a felony.

"The Internet and e-mail are spreading this scam far and fast," said Jodie Bernstein, Director of the FTC's Bureau of Consumer Protection. "America Online reports that credit repair schemes represent one of the biggest categories of unsolicited commercial e-mail or spam. Fourteen of the FTC defendants advertised their services on Internet Web pages. These scams target very vulnerable consumers. They prey on people who are plagued by poor credit—people who may be desperate to develop a clean credit history so they can get a loan, get a job, or buy a car."

"This type of crime creates several victims," said Drew Edmondson, Oklahoma Attorney General and chairman of the NAAG Consumer Protection Committee. "The unsuspecting consumers who only want to repair their credit are victimized, as are the businesses who grant credit based on falsified information and then are forced to increase prices. We as consumers must pay the higher prices to make up for their losses. The law enforcement actions already filed are just the tip of the iceberg compared to the suspected number of file segregation scams circulating the Internet and newspapers today. I speak for all attorneys general when I say we will continue to pursue these criminals."

Bernstein added, "File segregation scammers tell consumers they can show them how to create a whole, new credit identity. They tell them their scheme is legal. In short, they lie to consumers, take their money, and turn them into lawbreakers. The fact is that it takes time to rebuild a good credit reputation. There is no legal way for consumers to alter their credit identification to conceal adverse information that is accurate and timely."

In the cases announced today, the firms in question advertised their services in newspapers, magazines, and on Internet sites. Using claims such as, "Erase bad credit," "Anyone can have a new credit file instantly overnight," and "Start all over again with brand new credit," the companies offered to show consumers how to develop new credit identities through file segregation.

Many of the ads claim that, "It's 100% Legal," or "It's not only legal, it's your right." For fees ranging from $29.95 to $200, the companies offer to sell consumers the instructions they need to apply to the Internal Revenue Service for employer or taxpayer identification numbers.

Consumers were typically counseled to use the new I.D. number in place of their Social Security number when applying for credit. They frequently were given advice about how to develop whole new credit profiles by doing such things as getting new driver's licenses using the new identification number and advised about places that would give consumers "starter credit" using the new number. Using a false Social Security number—such as a taxpayer I.D. number—to apply for credit violates federal law and has been prosecuted vigorously by the IRS and U.S. Attorneys.

Fourteen complaints filed by the FTC, along with another three filed by the Justice Department at the FTC's request, allege violations of the Credit Repair Organizations Act and the FTC Act. The FTC and the Justice Department have asked U. S. District Courts to permanently enjoin the illegal claims and order consumer redress or civil penalties for the defendants.

In addition, 21cases were announced by the Attorneys General of Arizona, California, Connecticut, Delaware, Illinois, Kentucky, Minnesota, Missouri, Nevada, North Carolina, Ohio, Oklahoma, Oregon, and Pennsylvania. Finally, the Treasury Inspector General for Tax Administration (formerly the IRS Internal Security Division) announced that criminal search warrants had been executed in an additional five cases. Other law enforcement agencies participating in the joint effort, but not announcing cases today, include the Orange County and Santa Clara County, California, District Attorneys; the San Diego, California, City Attorney; the United States Attorney for the District of New Jersey; and the Massachusetts, Michigan, Tennessee, and Wisconsin Attorneys General.

These cases were announced in conjunction with National Consumer Protection Week, a nationwide consumer education and law enforcement initiative sponsored by a broad coalition of public and private consumer protection advocates including the FTC, National Association of Attorneys General, U. S. Postal Inspection Service, National Association of Consumer Agency Administrators, National Consumers League, and the American Association of Retired Persons. Activities across the country will focus on five different types of credit fraud that can affect consumers in every walk of life. The week, whose theme is "Credit Fraud — Know the Rules, Use the Tools," aims to raise awareness about credit scams and teach consumers how to protect themselves.

NOTE: The Commission files a complaint when it has "reason to believe" that the law has been or is being violated, and it appears to the Commission that a proceeding is in the public interest. The complaint is not a finding or ruling that the defendant has actually violated the law. The case will be decided by the court.

Copies of complaints and consumer education materials about fraud are available from the FTC's web site at `www.ftc.gov` and also from the FTC's Consumer Response Center, Room 130, 600 Pennsylvania Avenue, N.W., Washington, D.C. 20580; (202) FTC-HELP ((202) 382-4357); TDD for the hearing impaired (202) 326-2502.

A victim speaks

May 23, 1999

My husband's two major credit cards were taken from his wallet very selectively on Saturday, May 22. The cards were inside a very small wallet which was located in a box in the car. It was not clearly visible and the car was locked. The car was parked in a school parking lot while my husband and daughter were at a soccer game. Within two hours, the thief had generated a fake ID with a fake address and phone number. My husband's driver's license was not taken but his Social Security number could have been stolen. He had a telephone calling card in the wallet, too, which was not taken. Within three hours, the Discover credit card security department called and left a message at our home about suspicious purchases. Nonetheless, the thief managed to spend over $6800 on high-end laptop computers in less than four hours!

We don't yet know the extent of the financial damage as we do not know if checks have been written or new accounts opened in my husband's name. We are going to call all the credit bureaus tomorrow. We have notified all the card companies and our credit union. We believe the thief attempted to use our Visa card but was rejected because the balance went over our limit. I was shocked to find all local authorities do nothing about this type of crime. They even sigh about filing a police report. I am not the type to give up, however, and I plan to take this thing as far as I can. I will involve media if given the opportunity.

As soon as I saw that I had to take the matter in my own hands, I called the credit card company and got the details of the purchases made. I went to each and every store (a total of 3 so far) and spoke with *everyone* involved. I took notes on just what each person told me. I asked questions about surveillance and I asked for copies of all of the thief's transactions, including his signature. Through my work today (with the help of my 12-year-old daughter), I found eight people who can match the physical identification of the imposter! One lady noted very fine details about the man's face and clothing!

My next step is to notify the appropriate fraud units locally. The theft of the cards occurred in the Northern Virginia area while the fraud occurred some 15+ miles away in Maryland (two different suburbs there). I managed to corroborate the stories of the different CompUSA and Circuit City employees. I have details for the local authorities to go on. I am going to *insist* that action be taken by ALL. I have had enough of the "Gee, ma'am, you have to consider the extent of this problem. It is the credit card company's responsibility to investigate." *What???!!!* The credit card company is based in Delaware! You mean I can't get someone here to look into *local* crime?! "But, ma'am, you don't understand...we get hundreds of these cases a week." *Exactly* my point! Why can't I work as one to help stop this? This imposter isn't *expecting* anyone to follow his trail. He *knows* he can get away with it. He will continue to stalk potential victims at family sports events. He will continue to tarnish the credit of others. I, on the other hand, plan to stop him as best I can. I have alerted all the stores he apparently frequents. Someone at one store prevented him from charging an additional $3,000 because he said something "just didn't fit." The salesperson asked a lot of questions and it scared the fellow off. The salesperson has "seen the guy before." Unfortunately, one salesperson allowed a sale with a fake ID. The salesperson did say that when she asked for his address, he had to pull his fake ID out first! The salesperson at the other store said that the zip code did not match the city but the thief said, "I forgot it...I just moved here." Unfortunately, the salesperson did not match up the address the thief gave with the one written on the fake ID. If he had, he would have found that the zip code was ok but the thief stupidly messed up the city!

I have found eight people who could identify this man. I have the faked signatures of the thief. I have been told that at one of the stores, the man is on the surveillance tape without doubt. If the authorities choose to do nothing now, I will implore the media to take my case to the public. I expect such super leads to be followed to the fullest. I expect the local businesses to be alerted by the police so that this man can be apprehended when he tries to commit the same crime against someone else.

Will it all pan out? I don't know. I spent time gathering the evidence in order to protect myself and others. If apathy prevails, I will become more vocal. Police are aware of this crime daily. They even know where it occurs. They have washed their own hands of any responsibility to resolve it, however. They even imply that the credit card authorities will not be interested because it isn't "corporate theft" or some other high-level crime. They are basically saying, "Sorry, ma'am, there isn't a thing you can do really." Hogwash! I can make fliers. I can contact local businesses that have yet to be targeted. I can write to my lawmakers. I can contact the media. Don't expect me to "lie down and take it." As many report on the Web sites like this, the nightmare is not always over when you take steps.

Why should I have the police department's attitude? It is my credit that is being blasted, not theirs! Tenacity—I have that, too!

I plan to call the local county school security regarding the need for more security even when school is not in session. I began to think that surveillance should be increased during sports events where people are being scrutinized by career criminals. In this time of high school violence, this increased security should be a priority!

I plan to call the CompUSA folks, also. I am *very* unhappy that a second check of ID was not initiated with such an expensive purchase. Clearly, the criminal made a stupid mistake that the salesperson did not pick up on. Part of the perpetuation of this crime is caused by careless employees. Evidence of an ID is *not* enough. Training must be done as in the case with the Circuit City employee who used his training to prevent a would-be criminal from pursuing his crime! Employees must see that fake IDs are prevalent and blind acceptance of this should *not* be tolerated. The salespeople should be nosey and ask just the right questions. I say go with your "gut instinct." In most cases it will not let you down given other key signs.

The public must be educated further about the lack of follow-up in white collar crime. I doubt many know how little the police will do in such cases. I apparently missed some of the news shows featuring this problem in the past. I think more attention should be given to the matter. I plan to let others know about our recent victimization in the school parking lot by way of a flier (factual but asking a lot of questions). I want this particular individual's "playing field" to be decreased. I will be careful not to leave my identity as I want to be safe not sorry.

I plan to call others who might offer help to expand public knowledge quickly. At least the store employees I spoke with will be on their toes as I spoke with them in depth about this person's tactics. While I don't want anyone fired over the matter, I do want careful scrutiny in such sales. The purchases our identity thief made were the largest of the day at the stores he visited. More red flags should be going up. Why aren't they? I need some answers to feel secure with credit card ownership. Businesses should be held accountable, too.

Part 3

Appendices

Appendix A

The Fair Credit Reporting Act

As a public service, the staff of the Federal Trade Commission (FTC) has prepared the following complete text of the Fair Credit Reporting Act (FCRA), 15 U.S.C. § 1681 *et seq.* Although staff generally followed the format of the U.S. Code as published by the Government Printing Office, the format of this text does differ in minor ways from the Code (and from West's U.S. Code Annotated). For example, this version uses FCRA section numbers (§§ 601-625) in the headings. (The relevant U.S. Code citation is included with each section heading and each reference to the FCRA in the text.)

This version of the FCRA is complete as of July 1999. It includes the amendments to the FCRA set forth in the Consumer Credit Reporting Reform Act of 1996 (Public Law 104-208, the Omnibus Consolidated Appropriations Act for Fiscal Year 1997, Title II, Subtitle D, Chapter 1), Section 311 of the Intelligence Authorization for Fiscal Year 1998 (Public Law 105-107), and the Consumer Reporting Employment Clarification Act of 1998 (Public Law 105-347).

Table of Contents

§ 606 Disclosure of investigative consumer reports
§ 607 Compliance procedures
§ 608 Disclosures to governmental agencies
§ 609 Disclosures to consumers
§ 610 Conditions and form of disclosure to consumers
§ 611 Procedure in case of disputed accuracy
§ 612 Charges for certain disclosures
§ 613 Public record information for employment purposes
§ 614 Restrictions on investigative consumer reports
§ 615 Requirements on users of consumer reports
§ 616 Civil liability for willful noncompliance
§ 617 Civil liability for negligent noncompliance
§ 618 Jurisdiction of courts; limitation of actions
§ 619 Obtaining information under false pretenses
§ 620 Unauthorized disclosures by officers or employees
§ 621 Administrative enforcement
§ 622 Information on overdue child support obligations
§ 623 Responsibilities of furnishers of information to consumer reporting agencies
§ 624 Relation to State laws
§ 625 Disclosures to FBI for counterintelligence purposes

§ 601. Short title

This title may be cited as the Fair Credit Reporting Act.

§ 602. Congressional findings and statement of purpose [15 U.S.C. §1681]

(a) Accuracy and fairness of credit reporting. The Congress makes the following findings:

> (1) The banking system is dependent upon fair and accurate credit reporting. Inaccurate credit reports directly impair the efficiency of the banking system, and unfair credit reporting methods undermine the public confidence which is essential to the continued functioning of the banking system.
>
> (2) An elaborate mechanism has been developed for investigating and evaluating the creditworthiness, credit standing, capacity, character, and general reputation of consumers.

(3) Consumer reporting agencies have assumed a vital role in assembling and evaluating consumer credit and other information on consumers.

(4) There is a need to insure that consumer reporting agencies exercise their grave responsibilities with fairness, impartiality, and a respect for the consumer's right to privacy.

(b) Reasonable procedures. It is the purpose of this title to require that consumer reporting agencies adopt reasonable procedures for meeting the needs of commerce for consumer credit, personnel, insurance, and other information in a manner which is fair and equitable to the consumer, with regard to the confidentiality, accuracy, relevancy, and proper utilization of such information in accordance with the requirements of this title.

§ 603. Definitions; rules of construction [15 U.S.C.§1681a]

(a) Definitions and rules of construction set forth in this section are applicable for the purposes of this title.

(b) The term "person" means any individual, partnership, corporation, trust, estate, cooperative, association, government or governmental subdivision or agency, or other entity.

(c) The term "consumer" means an individual.

(d) Consumer report.

(1) In general. The term "consumer report" means any written, oral, or other communication of any information by a consumer reporting agency bearing on a consumer's credit worthiness, credit standing, credit capacity, character, general reputation, personal characteristics, or mode of living which is used or expected to be used or collected in whole or in part for the purpose of serving as a factor in establishing the consumer's eligibility for

(A) credit or insurance to be used primarily for personal, family, or household purposes;

(B) employment purposes; or

(C) any other purpose authorized under section 604 [§ 1681b].

(2) Exclusions. The term "consumer report" doesn't include

(A) any
(i) report containing information solely as to transactions or experiences between the consumer and the person making the report;
(ii) communication of that information among persons related by common ownership or affiliated by corporate control; or
(iii) communication of other information among persons related by common ownership or affiliated by corporate control, if it is clearly and conspicuously disclosed to the consumer that the information may be communicated among such persons and the consumer is given the opportunity, before the time that the information is initially communicated, to direct that such information not be communicated among such persons;
(B) any authorization or approval of a specific extension of credit directly or indirectly by the issuer of a credit card or similar device;
(C) any report in which a person who has been requested by a third party to make a specific extension of credit directly or indirectly to a consumer conveys his or her decision with respect to such request, if the third party advises the consumer of the name and address of the person to whom the request was made, and such person makes the disclosures to the consumer required under section 615 [§ 1681m]; or
(D) a communication described in subsection (o).

(e) The term "investigative consumer report" means a consumer report or portion thereof in which information on a consumer's character, general reputation, personal characteristics, or mode of living is obtained through personal interviews with neighbors, friends, or associates of the consumer reported on or with others with whom he is acquainted or who may have knowledge concerning any such items of information. However, such information shall not include specific factual information on a consumer's credit record obtained directly from a creditor of the consumer or from a consumer reporting agency when such information was obtained directly from a creditor of the consumer or from the consumer.

(f) The term "consumer reporting agency" means any person which, for monetary fees, dues, or on a cooperative nonprofit basis, regularly engages in whole or in part in the practice of assembling or evaluating consumer credit information or other information on consumers for the purpose of furnishing consumer reports to third parties, and which uses any means or facility of interstate commerce for the purpose of preparing or furnishing consumer reports.

(g) The term "file," when used in connection with information on any consumer, means all of the information on that consumer recorded and retained by a consumer reporting agency regardless of how the information is stored.

(h) The term "employment purposes" when used in connection with a consumer report means a report used for the purpose of evaluating a consumer for employment, promotion, reassignment or retention as an employee.

(i) The term "medical information" means information or records obtained, with the consent of the individual to whom it relates, from licensed physicians or medical practitioners, hospitals, clinics, or other medical or medically related facilities.

(j) Definitions relating to child support obligations.

> (1) Overdue support. The term "overdue support" has the meaning given to such term in section 666(e) of title 42 [Social Security Act, 42 U.S.C. § 666(e)].
>
> (2) State or local child support enforcement agency. The term "State or local child support enforcement agency" means a State or local agency which administers a State or local program for establishing and enforcing child support obligations.

(k) Adverse action.

> (1) Actions included. The term "adverse action"
>
> > (A) has the same meaning as in section 701(d)(6) of the Equal Credit Opportunity Act; and

(B) means

(i) a denial or cancellation of, an increase in any charge for, or a reduction or other adverse or unfavorable change in the terms of coverage or amount of, any insurance, existing or applied for, in connection with the underwriting of insurance;

(ii) a denial of employment or any other decision for employment purposes that adversely affects any current or prospective employee;

(iii) a denial or cancellation of, an increase in any charge for, or any other adverse or unfavorable change in the terms of, any license or benefit described in section 604(a)(3)(D) [§ 1681b]; and

(iv) an action taken or determination that is

(I) made in connection with an application that was made by, or a transaction that was initiated by, any consumer, or in connection with a review of an account under section 604(a)(3)(F)(ii)[§ 1681b]; and

(II) adverse to the interests of the consumer.

(2) Applicable findings, decisions, commentary, and orders. For purposes of any determination of whether an action is an adverse action under paragraph (1)(A), all appropriate final findings, decisions, commentary, and orders issued under section 701(d)(6) of the Equal Credit Opportunity Act by the Board of Governors of the Federal Reserve System or any court shall apply.

(l) Firm offer of credit or insurance. The term "firm offer of credit or insurance" means any offer of credit or insurance to a consumer that will be honored if the consumer is determined, based on information in a consumer report on the consumer, to meet the specific criteria used to select the consumer for the offer, except that the offer may be further conditioned on one or more of the following:

(1) The consumer being determined, based on information in the consumer's application for the credit or insurance, to

meet specific criteria bearing on credit worthiness or insurability, as applicable, that are established

(A) before selection of the consumer for the offer; and

(B) for the purpose of determining whether to extend credit or insurance pursuant to the offer.

(2) Verification

(A) that the consumer continues to meet the specific criteria used to select the consumer for the offer, by using information in a consumer report on the consumer, information in the consumer's application for the credit or insurance, or other information bearing on the credit worthiness or insurability of the consumer; or

(B) of the information in the consumer's application for the credit or insurance, to determine that the consumer meets the specific criteria bearing on credit worthiness or insurability.

(3) The consumer furnishing any collateral that is a requirement for the extension of the credit or insurance that was

(A) established before selection of the consumer for the offer of credit or insurance; and

(B) disclosed to the consumer in the offer of credit or insurance.

(m) Credit or insurance transaction that is not initiated by the consumer. The term "credit or insurance transaction that is not initiated by the consumer" does not include the use of a consumer report by a person with which the consumer has an account or insurance policy, for purposes of

(1) reviewing the account or insurance policy; or

(2) collecting the account.

(n) State. The term "State" means any State, the Commonwealth of Puerto Rico, the District of Columbia, and any territory or possession of the United States.

(o) Excluded communications. A communication is described in this subsection if it is a communication

(1) that, but for subsection (d)(2)(D), would be an investigative consumer report;

(2) that is made to a prospective employer for the purpose of

(A) procuring an employee for the employer; or

(B) procuring an opportunity for a natural person to work for the employer;

(3) that is made by a person who regularly performs such procurement;

(4) that is not used by any person for any purpose other than a purpose described in subparagraph (A) or (B) of paragraph (2); and

(5) with respect to which

(A) the consumer who is the subject of the communication

(i) consents orally or in writing to the nature and scope of the communication, before the collection of any information for the purpose of making the communication;

(ii) consents orally or in writing to the making of the communication to a prospective employer, before the making of the communication; and

(iii) in the case of consent under clause (i) or (ii) given orally, is provided written confirmation of that consent by the person making the communication, not later than 3 business days after the receipt of the consent by that person;

(B) the person who makes the communication does not, for the purpose of making the communication, make any inquiry that if made by a prospective employer of the consumer who is the subject of the communication would violate any

applicable Federal or State equal employment opportunity law or regulation; and
(C) the person who makes the communication
(i) discloses in writing to the consumer who is the subject of the communication, not later than 5 business days after receiving any request from the consumer for such disclosure, the nature and substance of all information in the consumer's file at the time of the request, except that the sources of any information that is acquired solely for use in making the communication and is actually used for no other purpose, need not be disclosed other than under appropriate discovery procedures in any court of competent jurisdiction in which an action is brought; and
(ii) notifies the consumer who is the subject of the communication, in writing, of the consumer's right to request the information described in clause (i).

(p) Consumer reporting agency that compiles and maintains files on consumers on a nationwide basis. The term "consumer reporting agency that compiles and maintains files on consumers on a nationwide basis" means a consumer reporting agency that regularly engages in the practice of assembling or evaluating, and maintaining, for the purpose of furnishing consumer reports to third parties bearing on a consumer's credit worthiness, credit standing, or credit capacity, each of the following regarding consumers residing nationwide:

(1) Public record information.

(2) Credit account information from persons who furnish that information regularly and in the ordinary course of business.

§ 604. Permissible purposes of consumer reports [15 U.S.C. §1681b]

(a) In general. Subject to subsection (c), any consumer reporting agency may furnish a consumer report under the following circumstances and no other:

(1) In response to the order of a court having jurisdiction to issue such an order, or a subpoena issued in connection with proceedings before a Federal grand jury.

(2) In accordance with the written instructions of the consumer to whom it relates.

(3) To a person which it has reason to believe

(A) intends to use the information in connection with a credit transaction involving the consumer on whom the information is to be furnished and involving the extension of credit to, or review or collection of an account of, the consumer; or

(B) intends to use the information for employment purposes; or

(C) intends to use the information in connection with the underwriting of insurance involving the consumer; or

(D) intends to use the information in connection with a determination of the consumer's eligibility for a license or other benefit granted by a governmental instrumentality required by law to consider an applicant's financial responsibility or status; or

(E) intends to use the information, as a potential investor or servicer, or current insurer, in connection with a valuation of, or an assessment of the credit or prepayment risks associated with, an existing credit obligation; or

(F) otherwise has a legitimate business need for the information

(i) in connection with a business transaction that is initiated by the consumer; or

(ii) to review an account to determine whether the consumer continues to meet the terms of the account.

(4) In response to a request by the head of a State or local child support enforcement agency (or a State or local government official authorized by the head of such an agency), if the person making the request certifies to the consumer reporting agency that

(A) the consumer report is needed for the purpose of establishing an individual's capacity to make child support payments or determining the appropriate level of such payments;

(B) the paternity of the consumer for the child to which the obligation relates has been established or acknowledged by the consumer in accordance with State laws under which the obligation arises (if required by those laws);

(C) the person has provided at least 10 days' prior notice to the consumer whose report is requested, by certified or registered mail to the last known address of the consumer, that the report will be requested; and

(D) the consumer report will be kept confidential, will be used solely for a purpose described in subparagraph (A), and will not be used in connection with any other civil, administrative, or criminal proceeding, or for any other purpose.

(5) To an agency administering a State plan under Section 454 of the Social Security Act (42 U.S.C. § 654) for use to set an initial or modified child support award.

(b) Conditions for furnishing and using consumer reports for employment purposes.

(1) Certification from user. A consumer reporting agency may furnish a consumer report for employment purposes only if

(A) the person who obtains such report from the agency certifies to the agency that

(i) the person has complied with paragraph (2) with respect to the consumer report, and the person will comply with paragraph (3) with respect to the consumer report if paragraph (3) becomes applicable; and

(ii) information from the consumer report will not be used in violation of any applicable Federal or State equal employment opportunity law or regulation; and

(B) the consumer reporting agency provides with the report, or has previously provided, a summary of the consumer's rights under this title, as prescribed by the Federal Trade Commission under section 609(c)(3) [§ 1681g].

(2) Disclosure to consumer.

(A) In general. Except as provided in subparagraph (B), a person may not procure a consumer report, or cause a consumer report to be procured, for employment purposes with respect to any consumer, unless—

(i) a clear and conspicuous disclosure has been made in writing to the consumer at any time before the report is procured or caused to be procured, in a document that consists solely of the disclosure, that a consumer report may be obtained for employment purposes; and

(ii) the consumer has authorized in writing (which authorization may be made on the document referred to in clause (i)) the procurement of the report by that person.

(B) Application by mail, telephone,

computer, or other similar means. If a consumer described in subparagraph (C) applies for employment by mail, telephone, computer, or other similar means, at any time before a consumer report is procured or caused to be procured in connection with that application—

(i) the person who procures the consumer report on the consumer for employment purposes shall provide to the consumer, by oral, written, or electronic means, notice that a consumer report may be obtained for employment purposes, and a summary of the consumer's rights under section 615(a)(3); and

(ii) the consumer shall have consented, orally, in writing, or electronically to the procurement of the report by that person.

(C) Scope. Subparagraph (B) shall apply to a person procuring a consumer report on a consumer in connection with the consumer's application for employment only if—

(i) the consumer is applying for a position over which the Secretary of Transportation has the power to establish qualifications and maximum hours of service pursuant to the provisions of section 31502 of title 49, or a position subject to safety regulation by a State transportation agency; and

(ii) as of the time at which the person procures the report or causes the report to be procured the only interaction between the consumer and the person in connection with that employment application has been by mail, telephone, computer, or other similar means.

(3) Conditions on use for adverse actions.

(A) In general. Except as provided in subparagraph (B), in using a consumer report for employment purposes, before taking any adverse action based in whole or in part on the report, the person intending to take such adverse action shall provide to the consumer to whom the report relates—

(i) a copy of the report; and

(ii) a description in writing of the rights of the consumer under this title, as prescribed by the Federal Trade Commission under section 609(c)(3).

(B) Application by mail, telephone, computer, or other similar means.

(i) If a consumer described in subparagraph (C) applies for employment by mail, telephone, computer, or other similar means, and if a person who has procured a consumer report on the consumer for employment purposes takes adverse action on the employment application based in whole or in part on the report, then the person must provide to the consumer to whom the report relates, in lieu of the notices required under subparagraph (A) of this section and under section 615(a), within 3 business days of taking such action, an oral, written or electronic notification—

(I) that adverse action has been taken based in whole or in part on a consumer report received from a consumer reporting agency;

(II) of the name, address and telephone number of the consumer reporting agency that furnished the consumer report (including a toll-free telephone number established by the agency if the agency compiles and maintains files on consumers on a nation wide basis);

(III) that the consumer reporting agency did not make the decision to take the adverse action and is unable to provide to the consumer the specific reasons why the adverse action was taken; and

(IV) that the consumer may, upon providing proper identification, request a free copy of a report and may dispute with the consumer reporting agency the accuracy or completeness of any information in a report.

(ii) If, under clause (B)(i)(IV), the consumer requests a copy of a consumer report from the person who procured the report, then, within 3 business days of receiving the consumer's request, together with proper identification, the person must send or provide to the consumer a copy of a report and a copy of the consumer's rights as prescribed by the Federal Trade Commission under section 609(c)(3).

(C) Scope. Subparagraph (B) shall apply to a person procuring a consumer report on a consumer in connection with the consumer's application for employment only if—

(i) the consumer is applying for a position over which the Secretary of Transportation has the power to establish qualifications and maximum hours of service pursuant to the provisions of section 31502 of title 49, or a position subject to safety regulation by a State transportation agency; and

(ii) as of the time at which the person procures the report or causes the report to be procured the only interaction between the consumer and the person in connection with that employment application has been by mail, telephone, computer, or other similar means.

(4) Exception for national security investigations.

(A) In general. In the case of an agency or department of the United States Government which seeks to obtain and use a consumer report for employment purposes, paragraph (3) shall not apply to any adverse action by such agency or department which is based in part on such consumer report, if the head of such agency or department makes a written finding that—

(i) the consumer report is relevant to a national security investigation of such agency or department;

(ii) the investigation is within the jurisdiction of such agency or department;

(iii) there is reason to believe that compliance with paragraph (3) will—

(I) endanger the life or physical safety of any person;

(II) result in flight from prosecution;

(III) result in the destruction of, or tampering with, evidence relevant to the investigation;

(IV) result in the intimidation of a potential witness relevant to the investigation;

(V) result in the compromise of classified information; or

(VI) otherwise seriously jeopardize or unduly delay the investigation or another official proceeding.

(B) Notification of consumer upon conclusion of investigation. Upon the conclusion of a national security investigation described in subparagraph (A), or upon the determination that the exception under subparagraph (A) is no longer required for the reasons set forth in such subparagraph, the official exercising the authority in such subparagraph shall provide to the consumer who is the subject of the consumer report with regard to which such finding was made—

(i) a copy of such consumer report with any classified information redacted as necessary;

(ii) notice of any adverse action which is based, in part, on the consumer report; and

(iii) the identification with reasonable specificity of the nature of the investigation for which the consumer report was sought.

(C) Delegation by head of agency or department. For purposes of subparagraphs (A) and (B), the head of any agency or department of the United States Government may delegate his or her authorities under this paragraph to an official of such agency or department who has personnel security responsibilities and is a member of the Senior Executive Service or equivalent civilian or military rank.

(D) Report to the Congress. Not later than January 31 of each year, the head of each agency and department of the United States Government that exercised authority under this paragraph during the preceding year shall submit a report to the Congress on the number of times the department or agency exercised such authority during the year.

(E) Definitions. For purposes of this paragraph, the following definitions shall apply:

(i) Classified information. The term "classified information" means information that is protected from unauthorized disclosure under Executive Order No. 12958 or successor orders.

(ii) National security investigation. The term "national security investigation" means any official inquiry by an agency or department of the United States Government to determine the eligibility of a consumer to receive access or continued access to classified information or to determine whether classified information has been lost or compromised.

(c) Furnishing reports in connection with credit or insurance transactions that are not initiated by the consumer.

(1) In general. A consumer reporting agency may furnish a consumer report relating to any consumer pursuant to subparagraph (A) or (C) of subsection (a)(3) in connection with any credit or insurance transaction that is not initiated by the consumer only if

(A) the consumer authorizes the agency to provide such report to such person; or

(B) (i) the transaction consists of a firm offer of credit or insurance;

(ii) the consumer reporting agency has complied with subsection (e); and

(iii) there is not in effect an election by the consumer, made in accordance with subsection (e), to have the consumer's name and address excluded from lists of names provided by the agency pursuant to this paragraph.

(2) Limits on information received under paragraph (1)(B). A person may receive pursuant to paragraph (1)(B) only

(A) the name and address of a consumer;

(B) an identifier that is not unique to the consumer and that is used by the person solely for the purpose of verifying the identity of the consumer; and

(C) other information pertaining to a consumer that does not identify the relationship or experience of the consumer with respect to a particular creditor or other entity.

(3) Information regarding inquiries. Except as provided in section 609(a)(5) [§ 1681g], a consumer reporting agency

shall not furnish to any person a record of inquiries in connection with a credit or insurance transaction that is not initiated by a consumer.

(d) Reserved.

(e) Election of consumer to be excluded from lists.

(1) In general. A consumer may elect to have the consumer's name and address excluded from any list provided by a consumer reporting agency under subsection (c)(1)(B) in connection with a credit or insurance transaction that is not initiated by the consumer, by notifying the agency in accordance with paragraph (2) that the consumer does not consent to any use of a consumer report relating to the consumer in connection with any credit or insurance transaction that is not initiated by the consumer.

(2) Manner of notification. A consumer shall notify a consumer reporting agency under paragraph (1)

(A) through the notification system maintained by the agency under paragraph (5); or

(B) by submitting to the agency a signed notice of election form issued by the agency for purposes of this subparagraph.

(3) Response of agency after notification through system. Upon receipt of notification of the election of a consumer under paragraph (1) through the notification system maintained by the agency under paragraph (5), a consumer reporting agency shall

(A) inform the consumer that the election is effective only for the 2-year period following the election if the consumer does not submit to the agency a signed notice of election form issued by the agency for purposes of paragraph (2)(B); and

(B) provide to the consumer a notice of election form, if requested by the consumer, not later than 5 business days after receipt of the notification of the election through the system established under paragraph (5), in the

case of a request made at the time the
consumer provides notification through the
system.

(4) Effectiveness of election. An election of a consumer under paragraph (1)

(A) shall be effective with respect to a consumer reporting agency beginning 5 business days after the date on which the consumer notifies the agency in accordance with paragraph (2);

(B) shall be effective with respect to a consumer reporting agency

(i) subject to subparagraph (C), during the 2-year period beginning 5 business days after the date on which the consumer notifies the agency of the election, in the case of an election for which a consumer notifies the agency only in accordance with paragraph (2)(A); or

(ii) until the consumer notifies the agency under subparagraph (C), in the case of an election for which a consumer notifies the agency in accordance with paragraph (2)(B);

(C) shall not be effective after the date on which the consumer notifies the agency, through the notification system established by the agency under paragraph (5), that the election is no longer effective; and

(D) shall be effective with respect to each affiliate of the agency.

(5) Notification system.

(A) In general. Each consumer reporting agency that, under subsection (c)(1)(B), furnishes a consumer report in connection with a credit or insurance transaction that is not initiated by a consumer, shall

(i) establish and maintain a notification system, including a toll-free telephone number, which permits any consumer whose consumer report is maintained by the agency to notify the agency, with appropriate identification, of the consumer's election to have the consumer's name and address excluded from any such list of names and addresses provided by the agency for such a transaction; and

(ii) publish by not later than 365 days after the date of enactment of the Consumer Credit Reporting Reform Act of 1996, and not less than annually thereafter, in a publication of general circulation in the area served by the agency

(I) a notification that information in consumer files maintained by the agency may be used in connection with such transactions; and

(II) the address and toll-free telephone number for consumers to use to notify the agency of the consumer's election under clause (I).

(B) Establishment and maintenance as compliance. Establishment and maintenance of a notification system (including a toll-free telephone number) and publication by a consumer reporting agency on the agency's own behalf and on behalf of any of its affiliates in accordance with this paragraph is deemed to be compliance with this paragraph by each of those affiliates.

(6) Notification system by agencies that operate nationwide. Each consumer reporting agency that compiles and maintains files on consumers on a nationwide basis shall establish and maintain a notification system for purposes of paragraph (5) jointly with other such consumer reporting agencies.

(f) Certain use or obtaining of information prohibited. A person shall not use or obtain a consumer report for any purpose unless

(1) the consumer report is obtained for a purpose for which the consumer report is authorized to be furnished under this section; and

(2) the purpose is certified in accordance with section 607 [§ 1681e] by a prospective user of the report through a general or specific certification.

(g) Furnishing reports containing medical information. A consumer reporting agency shall not furnish for employment purposes, or in connection with a credit or insurance transaction, a consumer report that contains medical information about a consumer, unless the consumer consents to the furnishing of the report.

§ 605. Requirements relating to information contained in consumer reports [15 U.S.C. §1681c]

(a) Information excluded from consumer reports. Except as authorized under subsection (b) of this section, no consumer reporting agency may make any consumer report containing any of the following items of information:

(1) Cases under title 11 [United States Code] or under the Bankruptcy Act that, from the date of entry of the order for relief or the date of adjudication, as the case may be, antedate the report by more than 10 years.

(2) Civil suits, civil judgments, and records of arrest that from date of entry, antedate the report by more than seven years or until the governing statute of limitations has expired, whichever is the longer period.

(3) Paid tax liens which, from date of payment, antedate the report by more than seven years.

(4) Accounts placed for collection or charged to profit and loss which antedate the report by more than seven years.[(1)]

(5) Any other adverse item of information, other than records of convictions of crimes which antedates the report by more than seven years.

(b) Exempted cases. The provisions of subsection (a) of this section are not applicable in the case of any consumer credit report to be used in connection with

(1) a credit transaction involving, or which may reasonably

be expected to involve, a principal amount of $150,000 or more;

(2) the underwriting of life insurance involving, or which may reasonably be expected to involve, a face amount of $150,000 or more; or

(3) the employment of any individual at an annual salary which equals, or which may reasonably be expected to equal $75,000, or more.

(c) Running of reporting period.

(1) In general. The 7-year period referred to in paragraphs (4) and (6)[(2)] of subsection (a) shall begin, with respect to any delinquent account that is placed for collection (internally or by referral to a third party, whichever is earlier), charged to profit and loss, or subjected to any similar action, upon the expiration of the 180-day period beginning on the date of the commencement of the delinquency which immediately preceded the collection activity, charge to profit and loss, or similar action.

(2) Effective date. Paragraph (1) shall apply only to items of information added to the file of a consumer on or after the date that is 455 days after the date of enactment of the Consumer Credit Reporting Reform Act of 1996.

(d) Information required to be disclosed. Any consumer reporting agency that furnishes a consumer report that contains information regarding any case involving the consumer that arises under title 11, United States Code, shall include in the report an identification of the chapter of such title 11 under which such case arises if provided by the source of the information. If any case arising or filed under title 11, United States Code, is withdrawn by the consumer before a final judgment, the consumer reporting agency shall include in the report that such case or filing was withdrawn upon receipt of documentation certifying such withdrawal.

(e) Indication of closure of account by consumer. If a consumer reporting agency is notified pursuant to section 623(a)(4) [§ 1681s-2] that a credit account of a consumer was voluntarily closed by the consumer, the agency shall indicate that fact in any consumer report that includes information related to the account.

(f) Indication of dispute by consumer. If a consumer reporting agency is notified pursuant to section 623(a)(3) [§ 1681s-2] that information regarding a consumer who was furnished to the agency is disputed by the consumer, the agency shall indicate that fact in each consumer report that includes the disputed information.

§ 606. Disclosure of investigative consumer reports [15 U.S.C. §1681d]

(a) Disclosure of fact of preparation. A person may not procure or cause to be prepared an investigative consumer report on any consumer unless

(1) it is clearly and accurately disclosed to the consumer that an investigative consumer report including information as to his character, general reputation, personal characteristics and mode of living, whichever are applicable, may be made, and such disclosure

(A) is made in a writing mailed, or otherwise delivered, to the consumer, not later than three days after the date on which the report was first requested, and

(B) includes a statement informing the consumer of his right to request the additional disclosures provided for under subsection (b) of this section and the written summary of the rights of the consumer prepared pursuant to section 609(c) [§ 1681g]; and

(2) the person certifies or has certified to the consumer reporting agency that

(A) the person has made the disclosures to the consumer required by paragraph (1); and

(B) the person will comply with subsection (b).

(b) Disclosure on request of nature and scope of investigation. Any person who procures or causes to be prepared an investigative consumer report on any consumer shall, upon written request made by the consumer within a reasonable period of time after the receipt by him of the disclosure required by subsection (a)(1) of this section, make a complete and accurate disclosure of the nature and scope of the investigation requested. This disclosure shall be made in a writing mailed, or otherwise delivered, to the consumer not later than five days after the date on which the request for such disclosure was received from the consumer or such report was first requested, whichever is the later.

(c) Limitation on liability upon showing of reasonable procedures for compliance with provisions. No person may be held liable for any violation of subsection (a) or (b) of this section if he shows by a preponderance of the evidence that at the time of the violation he maintained reasonable procedures to assure compliance with subsection (a) or (b) of this section.

(d) Prohibitions.

(1) Certification. A consumer reporting agency shall not prepare or furnish investigative consumer report unless the agency has received a certification under subsection (a)(2) from the person who requested the report.

(2) Inquiries. A consumer reporting agency shall not make an inquiry for the purpose of preparing an investigative consumer report on a consumer for employment purposes if the making of the inquiry by an employer or prospective employer of the consumer would violate any applicable Federal or State equal employment opportunity law or regulation.

(3) Certain public record information. Except as otherwise provided in section 613 [§ 1681k], a consumer reporting agency shall not furnish an investigative consumer report that includes information that is a matter of public record and that relates to an arrest, indictment, conviction, civil judicial action, tax lien, or outstanding judgment, unless the agency has verified the accuracy of the information during the 30-day period ending on the date on which the report is furnished.

(4) Certain adverse information. A consumer reporting agency shall not prepare or furnish an investigative consumer report on a consumer that contains information that is adverse to the interest of the consumer and that is obtained through a personal interview with a neighbor, friend, or associate of the consumer or with another person with whom the consumer is acquainted or who has knowledge of such item of information, unless

(A) the agency has followed reasonable procedures to obtain confirmation of the information, from an additional source that has independent and direct knowledge of the information; or

(B) the person interviewed is the best possible source of the information.

§ 607. Compliance procedures [15 U.S.C. § 1681e]

(a) Identity and purposes of credit users. Every consumer reporting agency shall maintain reasonable procedures designed to avoid violations of section 605 [§ 1681c] and to limit the furnishing of consumer reports to the purposes listed under section 604 [§ 1681b] of this title. These procedures shall require that prospective users of the information identify themselves, certify the purposes for which the information is sought, and certify that the information will be used for no other purpose. Every consumer reporting agency shall make a reasonable effort to verify the identity of a new prospective user and the uses certified by such prospective user prior to furnishing such user a consumer report. No consumer reporting agency may furnish a consumer report to any person if it has reasonable grounds for believing that the consumer report will not be used for a purpose listed in section 604 [§ 1681b] of this title.

(b) Accuracy of report. Whenever a consumer reporting agency prepares a consumer report it shall follow reasonable procedures to assure maximum possible accuracy of the information concerning the individual about whom the report relates.

(c) Disclosure of consumer reports by users allowed. A consumer reporting agency may not prohibit a user of a consumer report furnished by the agency on a consumer from disclosing the contents of the report to the consumer, if adverse action against the consumer has been taken by the user based in whole or in part on the report.

(d) Notice to users and furnishers of information.

(1) Notice requirement. A consumer reporting agency shall provide to any person

(A) who regularly and in the ordinary course of business furnishes information to the agency with respect to any consumer; or

(B) to whom a consumer report is provided by the agency; a notice of such person's responsibilities under this title.

(2) Content of notice. The Federal Trade Commission shall prescribe the content of notices under paragraph (1), and a consumer reporting agency shall be in compliance with this subsection if it provides a notice under paragraph (1) that is substantially similar to the Federal Trade Commission prescription under this paragraph.

(e) Procurement of consumer report for resale.

(1) Disclosure. A person may not procure a consumer report for purposes of reselling the report (or any information in the report) unless the person discloses to the consumer reporting agency that originally furnishes the report

(A) the identity of the end-user of the report (or information); and

(B) each permissible purpose under section 604 [§ 1681b] for which the report is furnished to the end-user of the report (or information).

(2) Responsibilities of procurers for resale. A person who procures a consumer report for purposes of reselling the report (or any information in the report) shall

(A) establish and comply with reasonable procedures designed to ensure that the report (or information) is resold by the person only for a purpose for which the report may be furnished under section 604 [§ 1681b], including by requiring that each person to which the report (or information) is resold and that resells or provides the report (or information) to any other person

(i) identifies each end user of the resold report (or information);

(ii) certifies each purpose for which the report (or information) will be used; and

(iii) certifies that the report (or information) will be used for no other purpose; and

(B) before reselling the report, make reasonable efforts to verify the identifications and certifications made under subparagraph (A).

(3) Resale of consumer report to a federal agency or department. Notwithstanding paragraph (1) or (2), a person who procures a consumer report for purposes of reselling the report (or any information in the report) shall not disclose the identity of the end-user of the report under paragraph (1) or (2) if—

(A) the end user is an agency or department of the United States Government which procures the report from the person for purposes of determining the eligibility of the consumer concerned to receive access or continued access to classified information (as defined in section 604(b)(4)(E)(i)); and

(B) the agency or department certifies in writing to the person reselling the report that nondisclosure is necessary to protect classified information or the safety of persons employed by or contracting with, or undergoing investigation for work or contracting with the agency or department.

§ 608. Disclosures to governmental agencies [15 U.S.C. §1681f]

Notwithstanding the provisions of section 604 [§ 1681b] of this title, a consumer reporting agency may furnish identifying information respecting any consumer, limited to his name, address, former addresses, places of employment, or former places of employment, to a governmental agency.

§ 609. Disclosures to consumers [15 U.S.C. §1681g]

(a) Information on file; sources; report recipients. Every consumer reporting agency shall, upon request, and subject to 610(a)(1) [§ 1681h], clearly and accurately disclose to the consumer:

(1) All information in the consumer's file at the time of the request, except that nothing in this paragraph shall be construed to require a consumer reporting agency to disclose to a consumer any information concerning credit scores or any other risk scores or predictors relating to the consumer.

(2) The sources of the information; except that the sources of information acquired solely for use in preparing an investigative consumer report and actually used for no other purpose need not be disclosed: provided, that in the event an action is brought under this title, such sources shall be available to the plaintiff under appropriate discovery procedures in the court in which the action is brought.

(3) (A) Identification of each person (including each end-user identified under section 607(e)(1) [§ 1681e]) that procured a consumer report

(i) for employment purposes, during the 2-year period preceding the date on which the request is made; or

(ii) for any other purpose, during the 1-year period preceding the date on which the request is made.

(B) An identification of a person under subparagraph (A) shall include

(i) the name of the person or, if applicable, the trade name (written in full) under which such person conducts business; and

(ii) upon request of the consumer, the address and telephone number of the person.

(C) Subparagraph (A) does not apply if—

(i) the end user is an agency or department of the United States Government that procures the report from the person for purposes of determining the eligibility of the consumer to whom the report relates to receive access or continued access to classified information (as defined in section 604(b)(4)(E)(i)); and

(ii) the head of the agency or department makes a written finding as prescribed under section 604(b)(4)(A).

(4) The dates, original payees, and amounts of any checks upon which is based any adverse characterization of the consumer, included in the file at the time of the disclosure.

(5) A record of all inquiries received by the agency during the 1-year period preceding the request that identified the consumer in connection with a credit or insurance transaction that was not initiated by the consumer.

(b) Exempt information. The requirements of subsection (a) of this section respecting the disclosure of sources of information and the recipients of consumer reports do not apply to information received or consumer reports furnished prior to the effective date of this title except to the extent that the matter involved is contained in the files of the consumer reporting agency on that date.

(c) Summary of rights required to be included with disclosure.

(1) Summary of rights. A consumer reporting agency shall provide to a consumer, with each written disclosure by the agency to the consumer under this section

(A) a written summary of all of the rights that the consumer has under this title; and

(B) in the case of a consumer reporting agency that compiles and maintains files on consumers on a nationwide basis, a toll-free telephone number established by the agency, at which personnel are accessible to consumers during normal business hours.

(2) Specific items required to be included. The summary of rights required under paragraph (1) shall include

(A) a brief description of this title and all rights of consumers under this title;

(B) an explanation of how the consumer may exercise the rights of the consumer under this title;

(C) a list of all Federal agencies responsible for enforcing any provision of this title and the address and any appropriate phone number of each such agency, in a form that will assist the consumer in selecting the appropriate agency;

(D) a statement that the consumer may have additional rights under State law and that the

consumer may wish to contact a State or local consumer protection agency or a State attorney general to learn of those rights; and
(E) a statement that a consumer reporting agency is not required to remove accurate derogatory information from a consumer's file, unless the information is outdated under section 605 [§ 1681c] or cannot be verified.

(3) Form of summary of rights. For purposes of this subsection and any disclosure by a consumer reporting agency required under this title with respect to consumers' rights, the Federal Trade Commission (after consultation with each Federal agency referred to in section 621(b) [§ 1681s]) shall prescribe the form and content of any such disclosure of the rights of consumers required under this title. A consumer reporting agency shall be in compliance with this subsection if it provides disclosures under paragraph (1) that are substantially similar to the Federal Trade Commission prescription under this paragraph.

(4) Effectiveness. No disclosures shall be required under this subsection until the date on which the Federal Trade Commission prescribes the form and content of such disclosures under paragraph (3).

§ 610. Conditions and form of disclosure to consumers [15 U.S.C. §1681h]

(a) In general.

(1) Proper identification. A consumer reporting agency shall require, as a condition of making the disclosures required under section 609 [§ 1681g], that the consumer furnish proper identification.

(2) Disclosure in writing. Except as provided in subsection (b), the disclosures required to be made under section 609 [§ 1681g] shall be provided under that section in writing.

(b) Other forms of disclosure.

(1) In general. If authorized by a consumer, a consumer reporting agency may make the disclosures required under 609 [§ 1681g]

(A) other than in writing; and

(B) in such form as may be

(i) specified by the consumer in accordance with paragraph (2); and

(ii) available from the agency.

(2) Form. A consumer may specify pursuant to paragraph (1) that disclosures under section 609 [§ 1681g] shall be made

(A) in person, upon the appearance of the consumer at the place of business of the consumer reporting agency where disclosures are regularly provided, during normal business hours, and on reasonable notice;

(B) by telephone, if the consumer has made a written request for disclosure by telephone;

(C) by electronic means, if available from the agency; or

(D) by any other reasonable means that is available from the agency.

(c) Trained personnel. Any consumer reporting agency shall provide trained personnel to explain to the consumer any information furnished to him pursuant to section 609 [§ 1681g] of this title.

(d) Persons accompanying consumer. The consumer shall be permitted to be accompanied by one other person of his choosing, who shall furnish reasonable identification. A consumer reporting agency may require the consumer to furnish a written statement granting permission to the consumer reporting agency to discuss the consumer's file in such person's presence.

(e) Limitation of liability. Except as provided in sections 616 and 617 [§§ 1681n and 1681o] of this title, no consumer may bring any action or proceeding in the nature of defamation, invasion of privacy, or negligence with respect to the reporting of information against any consumer reporting agency, any user of information, or any person who furnishes information to a consumer reporting agency, based on information disclosed pursuant to section 609, 610, or 615 [§§ 1681g, 1681h, or 1681m] of this title or based on information disclosed by a user of a consumer report to or for a consumer against whom the user has taken adverse action, based in whole or in part on the report, except as to false information furnished with malice or willful intent to injure such consumer.

§ 611. Procedure in case of disputed accuracy [15 U.S.C. §1681i]

(a) Reinvestigations of disputed information.

(1) Reinvestigation required.

(A) In general. If the completeness or accuracy of any item of information contained in a consumer's file at a consumer reporting agency is disputed by the consumer and the consumer notifies the agency directly of such dispute, the agency shall reinvestigate free of charge and record the current status of the disputed information, or delete the item from the file in accordance with paragraph (5), before the end of the 30-day period beginning on the date on which the agency receives the notice of the dispute from the consumer.

(B) Extension of period to reinvestigate. Except as provided in subparagraph (C), the 30-day period described in subparagraph (A) may be extended for not more than 15 additional days if the consumer reporting agency receives information from the consumer during that 30-day period that is relevant to the reinvestigation.

(C) Limitations on extension of period to reinvestigate. Subparagraph (B) shall not apply to any reinvestigation in which, during the 30-day period described in subparagraph (A), the information that is the subject of the reinvestigation is found to be inaccurate or incomplete or the consumer reporting agency determines that the information cannot be verified.

(2) Prompt notice of dispute to furnisher of information.

(A) In general. Before the expiration of the 5-business-day period beginning on the date on which a consumer reporting agency receives notice of a dispute from any consumer in accordance with paragraph (1), the agency shall provide notification of the dispute to any person who provided any item of information in dispute, at the address and in the manner established with the person. The notice shall include all relevant information regarding the dispute that the agency has received from the consumer.

(B) Provision of other information from consumer. The consumer reporting agency shall promptly provide to the person who provided the information in dispute all relevant information regarding the dispute that is received by the agency from the consumer after the period referred to in subparagraph (A) and before the end of the period referred to in paragraph (1)(A).

(3) Determination that dispute is frivolous or irrelevant.

(A) In general. Notwithstanding paragraph (1), a consumer reporting agency may terminate a reinvestigation of information disputed by a consumer under that paragraph if the agency reasonably determines that the dispute by the consumer is frivolous or irrelevant, including by reason of a failure by a consumer to provide sufficient information to investigate the disputed information.

(B) Notice of determination. Upon making any determination in accordance with subparagraph (A) that a dispute is frivolous or irrelevant, a consumer reporting agency shall notify the consumer of such determination not later than 5 business days after making such determination, by mail or, if authorized by the consumer for that purpose, by any other means available to the agency.

(C) Contents of notice. A notice under subparagraph (B) shall include

(i) the reasons for the determination under subparagraph (A); and

(ii) identification of any information required to investigate the disputed information, which may consist of a standardized form describing the general nature of such information.

(4) Consideration of consumer information. In conducting any reinvestigation under paragraph (1) with respect to disputed information in the file of any consumer, the consumer reporting agency shall review and consider all relevant information submitted by the consumer in the period described in paragraph (1)(A) with respect to such disputed information.

(5) Treatment of inaccurate or unverifiable information.

(A) In general. If, after any reinvestigation under paragraph (1) of any information disputed by a consumer, an item of the information is found to be inaccurate or incomplete or cannot be verified, the consumer reporting agency shall promptly delete that item of information from the consumer's file or modify that item of information, as appropriate, based on the results of the reinvestigation.

(B) Requirements relating to reinsertion of previously deleted material.

(i) Certification of accuracy of information. If any information is deleted from a consumer's file pursuant to subparagraph (A), the information may not be reinserted in the file by the consumer reporting agency unless the person who furnishes the information certifies that the information is complete and accurate.

(ii) Notice to consumer. If any information that has been deleted from a consumer's file pursuant to subparagraph (A) is reinserted in the file, the consumer reporting agency shall notify the consumer of the reinsertion in writing not later than 5 business days after the reinsertion or, if authorized by the consumer for that purpose, by any other means available to the agency.

(iii) Additional information. As part of, or in addition to, the notice under clause (ii), a consumer reporting agency shall provide to a consumer in writing not later than 5 business days after the date of the reinsertion

(I) a statement that the disputed information has been reinserted;

(II) the business name and address of any furnisher of information contacted and the telephone number of such furnisher, if reasonably available, or of any furnisher of information that contacted the consumer reporting agency, in connection with the reinsertion of such information; and

(III) a notice that the consumer has the right to add a statement to the consumer's file disputing the accuracy or completeness of the disputed information.

(C) Procedures to prevent reappearance. A consumer reporting agency shall maintain reasonable procedures designed to prevent the reappearance in a consumer's file, and in consumer reports on the consumer, of information that is deleted pursuant to this paragraph (other than information that is reinserted in accordance with subparagraph (B)(i)).

(D) Automated reinvestigation system. Any consumer reporting agency that compiles and maintains files on consumers on a nationwide basis shall implement an automated system through which furnishers of information to that consumer reporting agency may report the results of a reinvestigation that finds incomplete or inaccurate information in a consumer's file to other such consumer reporting agencies.

(6) Notice of results of reinvestigation.

(A) In general. A consumer reporting agency shall provide written notice to a consumer of the results of a reinvestigation under this subsection not later than 5 business days after the completion of the reinvestigation, by mail or, if authorized by the consumer for that purpose, by other means available to the agency.

(B) Contents. As part of, or in addition to, the notice under subparagraph (A), a consumer reporting agency shall provide to a consumer in writing before the expiration of the 5-day period referred to in subparagraph (A)

(i) a statement that the reinvestigation is completed;

(ii) a consumer report that is based upon the consumer's file as that file is revised as a result of the reinvestigation;

(iii) a notice that, if requested by the consumer, a description of the procedure used to determine the accuracy and completeness of the information shall be provided to the consumer by the agency, including the business name and address of any furnisher of information contacted in connection with such information and the telephone number of such furnisher, if reasonably available;

(iv) a notice that the consumer has the right to add a statement to the consumer's file disputing the accuracy or completeness of the information; and

(v) a notice that the consumer has the right to request under subsection (d) that the consumer reporting agency furnish notifications under that subsection.

(7) Description of reinvestigation procedure. A consumer reporting agency shall provide to a consumer a description referred to in paragraph (6)(B)(iii) by not later than 15 days after receiving a request from the consumer for that description.

(8) Expedited dispute resolution. If a dispute regarding an item of information in a consumer's file at a consumer reporting agency is resolved in accordance with paragraph (5)(A) by the deletion of the disputed information by not later than 3 business days after the date on which the agency receives notice of the dispute from the consumer in accordance with paragraph (1)(A), then the agency shall not be required to comply with paragraphs (2), (6), and (7) with respect to that dispute if the agency

(A) provides prompt notice of the deletion to the consumer by telephone;

(B) includes in that notice, or in a written notice that accompanies a confirmation and consumer report provided in accordance with subparagraph (C), a statement of the consumer's right to request under subsection (d) that the agency furnish notifications under that subsection; and

(C) provides written confirmation of the deletion and a copy of a consumer report on the consumer that is based on the consumer's file after the deletion, not later than 5 business days after making the deletion.

(b) Statement of dispute. If the reinvestigation does not resolve the dispute, the consumer may file a brief statement setting forth the nature of the dispute. The consumer reporting agency may limit such statements to not more

than one hundred words if it provides the consumer with assistance in writing a clear summary of the dispute.
(c) Notification of consumer dispute in subsequent consumer reports. Whenever a statement of a dispute is filed, unless there is reasonable grounds to believe that it is frivolous or irrelevant, the consumer reporting agency shall, in any subsequent consumer report containing the information in question, clearly note that it is disputed by the consumer and provide either the consumer's statement or a clear and accurate codification or summary thereof.
(d) Notification of deletion of disputed information. Following any deletion of information which is found to be inaccurate or whose accuracy can no longer be verified or any notation as to disputed information, the consumer reporting agency shall, at the request of the consumer, furnish notification that the item has been deleted or the statement, codification or summary pursuant to subsection (b) or (c) of this section to any person specifically designated by the consumer who has within two years prior thereto received a consumer report for employment purposes, or within six months prior thereto received a consumer report for any other purpose, which contained the deleted or disputed information.

§ 612. Charges for certain disclosures [15 U.S.C. §1681j]

(a) Reasonable charges allowed for certain disclosures.

(1) In general. Except as provided in subsections (b), (c), and (d), a consumer reporting agency may impose a reasonable charge on a consumer

(A) for making a disclosure to the consumer pursuant to section 609 [§ 1681g], which charge
(i) shall not exceed $8; and
(ii) shall be indicated to the consumer before making the disclosure; and
(B) for furnishing, pursuant to 611(d) [§ 1681i], following a reinvestigation under section 611(a) [§ 1681i], a statement, codification, or summary to a person designated by the consumer under that

section after the 30-day period beginning on the date of notification of the consumer under paragraph (6) or (8) of section 611(a) [§ 1681i] with respect to the reinvestigation, which charge

(i) shall not exceed the charge that the agency would impose on each designated recipient for a consumer report; and

(ii) shall be indicated to the consumer before furnishing such information.

(2) Modification of amount. The Federal Trade Commission shall increase the amount referred to in paragraph (1)(A)(I) on January 1 of each year, based proportionally on changes in the Consumer Price Index, with fractional changes rounded to the nearest fifty cents.

(b) Free disclosure after adverse notice to consumer. Each consumer reporting agency that maintains a file on a consumer shall make all disclosures pursuant to section 609 [§ 1681g] without charge to the consumer if, not later than 60 days after receipt by such consumer of a notification pursuant to section 615 [§ 1681m], or of a notification from a debt collection agency affiliated with that consumer reporting agency stating that the consumer's credit rating may be or has been adversely affected, the consumer makes a request under section 609 [§ 1681g].

(c) Free disclosure under certain other circumstances. Upon the request of the consumer, a consumer reporting agency shall make all disclosures pursuant to section 609 [§ 1681g] once during any 12-month period without charge to that consumer if the consumer certifies in writing that the consumer

(1) is unemployed and intends to apply for employment in the 60-day period beginning on the date on which the certification is made;

(2) is a recipient of public welfare assistance; or

(3) has reason to believe that the file on the consumer at the agency contains inaccurate information due to fraud.

(d) Other charges prohibited. A consumer reporting agency shall not impose any charge on a consumer for providing any notification required by this title or making any disclosure required by this title, except as authorized by subsection (a).

§ 613. Public record information for employment purposes [15 U.S.C. §1681k]

(a) In general. A consumer reporting agency which furnishes a consumer report for employment purposes and which for that purpose compiles and reports items of information on consumers which are matters of public record and are likely to have an adverse effect upon a consumer's ability to obtain employment shall

(1) at the time such public record information is reported to the user of such consumer report, notify the consumer of the fact that public record information is being reported by the consumer reporting agency, together with the name and address of the person to whom such information is being reported; or

(2) maintain strict procedures designed to insure that whenever public record information which is likely to have an adverse effect on a consumer's ability to obtain employment is reported it is complete and up to date. For purposes of this paragraph, items of public record relating to arrests, indictments, convictions, suits, tax liens, and outstanding judgments shall be considered up to date if the current public record status of the item at the time of the report is reported.

(b) Exemption for national security investigations. Subsection (a) does not apply in the case of an agency or department of the United States Government that seeks to obtain and use a consumer report for employment purposes, if the head of the agency or department makes a written finding as prescribed under section 604(b)(4)(A).

§ 614. Restrictions on investigative consumer reports [15 U.S.C. §1681l]

Whenever a consumer reporting agency prepares an investigative consumer report, no adverse information in the consumer report (other than information which is a matter of public record) may be included in a subsequent consumer report unless such adverse information has been verified in the process of making such subsequent consumer report, or the adverse information was received within the three-month period preceding the date the subsequent report is furnished.

§ 615. Requirements on users of consumer reports [15 U.S.C. §1681m]

(a) Duties of users taking adverse actions on the basis of information contained in consumer reports. If any person takes any adverse action with respect to any consumer that is based in whole or in part on any information contained in a consumer report, the person shall

(1) provide oral, written, or electronic notice of the adverse action to the consumer;

(2) provide to the consumer orally, in writing, or electronically

(A) the name, address, and telephone number of the consumer reporting agency (including a toll-free telephone number established by the agency if the agency compiles and maintains files on consumers on a nationwide basis) that furnished the report to the person; and

(B) a statement that the consumer reporting agency did not make the decision to take the adverse action and is unable to provide the consumer the specific reasons why the adverse action was taken; and

(3) provide to the consumer an oral, written, or electronic notice of the consumer's right

(A) to obtain, under section 612 [§ 1681j], a free copy of a consumer report on the consumer from the consumer reporting agency referred to in paragraph (2), which notice shall include an indication of the 60-day period under that section for obtaining such a copy; and

(B) to dispute, under section 611 [§ 1681i], with a consumer reporting agency the accuracy or completeness of any information in a consumer report furnished by the agency.

(b) Adverse action based on information obtained from third parties other than consumer reporting agencies.

(1) In general. Whenever credit for personal, family, or household purposes involving a consumer is denied or the charge for such credit is increased either wholly or partly because of information obtained from a person other than a consumer reporting agency bearing upon the consumer's credit worthiness, credit standing, credit capacity, character, general reputation, personal characteristics, or mode of living, the user of such information shall, within a reasonable period of time, upon the consumer's written request for the reasons for such adverse action received within sixty days after learning of such adverse action, disclose the nature of the information to the consumer. The user of such information shall clearly and accurately disclose to the consumer his right to make such written request at the time such adverse action is communicated to the consumer.

(2) Duties of person taking certain actions based on information provided by affiliate.

(A) Duties, generally. If a person takes an action described in subparagraph (B) with respect to a consumer, based in whole or in part on information described in subparagraph (C), the person shall

(i) notify the consumer of the action, including a statement that the consumer may obtain the information in accordance with clause (ii); and

(ii) upon a written request from the consumer received within 60 days after transmittal of the notice required by clause (I), disclose to the consumer the nature of the information upon which the action is based by not later than 30 days after receipt of the request.

(B) Action described. An action referred to in subparagraph (A) is an adverse action described in section 603(k)(1)(A) [§ 1681a], taken in connection with a transaction initiated by the consumer, or any adverse action described in clause (i) or (ii) of section 603(k)(1)(B) [§ 1681a].

(C) Information described. Information referred to in subparagraph (A)

(i) except as provided in clause (ii), is information that

(I) is furnished to the person taking the action by a person related by common ownership or affiliated by common corporate control to the person taking the action; and

(II) bears on the credit worthiness, credit standing, credit capacity, character, general reputation, personal characteristics, or mode of living of the consumer; and

(ii) does not include

(I) information solely as to transactions or experiences between the consumer and the person furnishing the information; or

(II) information in a consumer report.

(c) Reasonable procedures to assure compliance. No person shall be held liable for any violation of this section if he shows by a preponderance of the evidence that at the time of the alleged violation he maintained reasonable procedures to assure compliance with the provisions of this section.

(d) Duties of users making written credit or insurance solicitations on the basis of information contained in consumer files.

(1) In general. Any person who uses a consumer report on any consumer in connection with any credit or insurance transaction that is not initiated by the consumer, that is provided to that person under section 604(c)(1)(B) [§ 1681b], shall provide with each written solicitation made to the consumer regarding the transaction a clear and conspicuous statement that

(A) information contained in the consumer's consumer report was used in connection with the transaction;

(B) the consumer received the offer of credit or insurance because the consumer satisfied the criteria for credit worthiness or insurability under which the consumer was selected for the offer;

(C) if applicable, the credit or insurance may not be extended if, after the consumer responds to the offer, the consumer does not meet the criteria used to select the consumer for the offer or any applicable criteria bearing on credit worthiness or insurability or does not furnish any required collateral;

(D) the consumer has a right to prohibit information contained in the consumer's file with any consumer reporting agency from being used in connection with any credit or insurance transaction that is not initiated by the consumer; and

(E) the consumer may exercise the right referred to in subparagraph (D) by notifying a notification system established under section 604(e) [§ 1681b].

(2) Disclosure of address and telephone number. A statement under paragraph (1) shall include the address and toll-free telephone number of the appropriate notification system established under section 604(e) [§ 1681b].

(3) Maintaining criteria on file. A person who makes an offer of credit or insurance to a consumer under a credit or insurance transaction described in paragraph (1) shall maintain on file the criteria used to select the consumer to receive the offer, all criteria bearing on credit worthiness or insurability, as applicable, that are the basis for determining whether or not to extend credit or insurance pursuant to the offer, and any requirement for the furnishing of collateral as a condition of the extension of credit or insurance, until the expiration of the 3-year period beginning on the date on which the offer is made to the consumer.

(4) Authority of federal agencies regarding unfair or deceptive acts or practices not affected. This section is not intended to affect the authority of any Federal or State agency to enforce

a prohibition against unfair or deceptive acts or practices, including the making of false or misleading statements in connection with a credit or insurance transaction that is not initiated by the consumer.

§ 616. Civil liability for willful noncompliance [15 U.S.C. §1681n]

(a) In general. Any person who willfully fails to comply with any requirement imposed under this title with respect to any consumer is liable to that consumer in an amount equal to the sum of

1) (A) any actual damages sustained by the consumer as a result of the failure or damages of not less than $100 and not more than $1,000; or

(B) in the case of liability of a natural person for obtaining a consumer report under false pretenses or knowingly without a permissible purpose, actual damages sustained by the consumer as a result of the failure or $1,000, whichever is greater;

(2) such amount of punitive damages as the court may allow; and

(3) in the case of any successful action to enforce any liability under this section, the costs of the action together with reasonable attorney's fees as determined by the court.

(b) Civil liability for knowing noncompliance. Any person who obtains a consumer report from a consumer reporting agency under false pretenses or knowingly without a permissible purpose shall be liable to the consumer reporting agency for actual damages sustained by the consumer reporting agency or $1,000, whichever is greater.

(c) Attorney's fees. Upon a finding by the court that an unsuccessful pleading, motion, or other paper filed in connection with an action under this section was filed in bad faith or for purposes of harassment, the court shall award to the prevailing party attorney's fees reasonable in relation to the work expended in responding to the pleading, motion, or other paper.

§ 617. Civil liability for negligent noncompliance [15 U.S.C. §1681o]

(a) In general. Any person who is negligent in failing to comply with any requirement imposed under this title with respect to any consumer is liable to that consumer in an amount equal to the sum of

(1) any actual damages sustained by the consumer as a result of the failure;

(2) in the case of any successful action to enforce any liability under this section, the costs of the action together with reasonable attorney's fees as determined by the court.

(b) Attorney's fees. On a finding by the court that an unsuccessful pleading, motion, or other paper filed in connection with an action under this section was filed in bad faith or for purposes of harassment, the court shall award to the prevailing party attorney's fees reasonable in relation to the work expended in responding to the pleading, motion, or other paper.

§ 618. Jurisdiction of courts; limitation of actions [15 U.S.C. §1681p]

An action to enforce any liability created under this title may be brought in any appropriate United States district court without regard to the amount in controversy, or in any other court of competent jurisdiction, within two years from the date on which the liability arises, except that where a defendant has materially and willfully misrepresented any information required under this title to be disclosed to an individual and the information so misrepresented is material to the establishment of the defendant's liability to that individual under this title, the action may be brought at any time within two years after discovery by the individual of the misrepresentation.

§ 619. Obtaining information under false pretenses [15 U.S.C. §1681q]

Any person who knowingly and willfully obtains information on a consumer from a consumer reporting agency under false pretenses shall be fined under title 18, United States Code, imprisoned for not more than 2 years, or both.

§ 620. Unauthorized disclosures by officers or employees [15 U.S.C. §1681r]

Any officer or employee of a consumer reporting agency who knowingly and willfully provides information concerning an individual from the agency's files to a person not authorized to receive that information shall be fined under title 18, United States Code, imprisoned for not more than 2 years, or both.

§ 621. Administrative enforcement [15 U.S.C. §1681s]

(a) (1) Enforcement by Federal Trade Commission. Compliance with the requirements imposed under this title shall be enforced under the Federal Trade Commission Act [15 U.S.C. §§ 41 et seq.] by the Federal Trade Commission with respect to consumer reporting agencies and all other persons subject thereto, except to the extent that enforcement of the requirements imposed under this title is specifically committed to some other government agency under subsection (b) hereof. For the purpose of the exercise by the Federal Trade Commission of its functions and powers under the Federal Trade Commission Act, a violation of any requirement or prohibition imposed under this title shall constitute an unfair or deceptive act or practice in commerce in violation of section 5(a) of the Federal Trade Commission Act [15 U.S.C. § 45(a)] and shall be subject to enforcement by the Federal Trade Commission under section 5(b) thereof [15 U.S.C. § 45(b)] with respect to any consumer reporting agency or person subject to enforcement by the Federal Trade Commission pursuant to this subsection, irrespective of whether that person is engaged in commerce or meets any other jurisdictional tests in the Federal Trade Commission Act. The Federal Trade Commission shall have such procedural, investigative, and enforcement powers, including the power to issue procedural rules in enforcing compliance with the requirements imposed under this title and to require the filing of reports, the production of documents, and the appearance of witnesses as though the applicable terms and conditions of the Federal Trade Commission Act were part of this title. Any person violating any of the provisions of this title shall be subject to the penalties and entitled to the privileges and immunities provided in the Federal Trade Commission Act as though the applicable terms and provisions thereof were part of this title.

2) (A) In the event of a knowing violation, which constitutes a pattern or practice of violations of this title, the Commission

may commence a civil action to recover a civil penalty in a district court of the United States against any person that violates this title. In such action, such person shall be liable for a civil penalty of not more than $2,500 per violation.

(B) In determining the amount of a civil penalty under subparagraph (A), the court shall take into account the degree of culpability, any history of prior such conduct, ability to pay, effect on ability to continue to do business, and such other matters as justice may require.

(3) Notwithstanding paragraph (2), a court may not impose any civil penalty on a person for a violation of section 623(a)(1) [§ 1681s-2] unless the person has been enjoined from committing the violation, or ordered not to commit the violation, in an action or proceeding brought by or on behalf of the Federal Trade Commission, and has violated the injunction or order, and the court may not impose any civil penalty for any violation occurring before the date of the violation of the injunction or order.

(4) Neither the Commission nor any other agency referred to in subsection (b) may prescribe trade regulation rules or other regulations with respect to this title.

(b) Enforcement by other agencies. Compliance with the requirements imposed under this title with respect to consumer reporting agencies, persons who use consumer reports from such agencies, persons who furnish information to such agencies, and users of information that are subject to subsection (d) of section 615 [§ 1681m] shall be enforced under

(1) section 8 of the Federal Deposit Insurance Act [12 U.S.C. § 1818], in the case of

(A) national banks, and Federal branches and Federal agencies of foreign banks, by the Office of the Comptroller of the Currency;

(B) member banks of the Federal Reserve System (other than national banks), branches and agencies of foreign banks (other than Federal branches, Federal agencies, and insured State branches of foreign banks), commercial lending companies owned or controlled by foreign banks, and organizations operating under section 25 or 25(a) [25A] of the Federal Reserve Act [12 U.S.C. §§ 601 et seq., §§ 611 et seq], by the Board of Governors of the Federal Reserve System; and

(C) banks insured by the Federal Deposit Insurance Corporation (other than members of the Federal Reserve System) and insured State branches of foreign banks, by the Board of Directors of the Federal Deposit Insurance Corporation;

(2) section 8 of the Federal Deposit Insurance Act [12 U.S.C. § 1818], by the Director of the Office of Thrift Supervision, in the case of a savings association the deposits of which are insured by the Federal Deposit Insurance Corporation;

(3) the Federal Credit Union Act [12 U.S.C. §§ 1751 et seq.], by the Administrator of the National Credit Union Administration [National Credit Union Administration Board] with respect to any Federal credit union;

(4) subtitle IV of title 49 [49 U.S.C. §§ 10101 et seq.], by the Secretary of Transportation, with respect to all carriers subject to the jurisdiction of the Surface Transportation Board;

(5) the Federal Aviation Act of 1958 [49 U.S.C. Appx §§ 1301 et seq.], by the Secretary of Transportation with respect to any air carrier or foreign air carrier subject to that Act [49 U.S.C. Appx §§ 1301 et seq.]; and

(6) the Packers and Stockyards Act, 1921 [7 U.S.C. §§ 181 et seq.] (except as provided in section 406 of that Act [7 U.S.C. §§ 226 and 227]), by the Secretary of Agriculture with respect to any activities subject to that Act.

The terms used in paragraph (1) that are not defined in this title or otherwise defined in section 3(s) of the Federal Deposit Insurance Act (12 U.S.C. § 1813(s)) shall have the meaning given to them in section 1(b) of the International Banking Act of 1978 (12 U.S.C. § 3101).

(c) State action for violations.

(1) Authority of states. In addition to such other remedies as are provided under State law, if the chief law enforcement officer of a State, or an official or agency designated by a State, has reason to believe that any person has violated or is violating this title, the State

(A) may bring an action to enjoin such violation in any appropriate United States district court or in any other court of competent jurisdiction;

(B) subject to paragraph (5), may bring an action on behalf of the residents of the State to recover

(i) damages for which the person is liable to such residents under sections 616 and 617 [§§ 1681n and 1681o] as a result of the violation;

(ii) in the case of a violation of section 623(a) [§ 1681s-2], damages for which the person would, but for section 623(c) [§ 1681s-2], be liable to such residents as a result of the violation; or

(iii) damages of not more than $1,000 for each willful or negligent violation; and

(C) in the case of any successful action under subparagraph (A) or (B), shall be awarded the costs of the action and reasonable attorney fees as determined by the court.

(2) Rights of federal regulators. The State shall serve prior written notice of any action under paragraph (1) upon the Federal Trade Commission or the appropriate Federal regulator determined under subsection (b) and provide the Commission or appropriate Federal regulator with a copy of its complaint, except in any case in which such prior notice is not feasible, in which case the State shall serve such notice immediately upon instituting such action. The Federal Trade Commission or appropriate Federal regulator shall have the right

(A) to intervene in the action;

(B) upon so intervening, to be heard on all matters arising therein;

(C) to remove the action to the appropriate United States district court; and

(D) to file petitions for appeal.

(3) Investigatory powers. For purposes of bringing any action under this subsection, nothing in this subsection shall prevent the chief law enforcement officer, or an official or agency designated by a State, from exercising the powers conferred on the chief law enforcement officer or such official by the laws of such State to conduct investigations or to administer oaths or affirmations or to compel the attendance of witnesses or the production of documentary and other evidence.

(4) Limitation on state action while federal action pending. If the Federal Trade Commission or the appropriate Federal regulator has instituted a civil action or an administrative action under section 8 of the Federal Deposit Insurance Act for a violation of this title, no State may, during the pendency of such action, bring an action under this section against any defendant named in the complaint of the Commission or the appropriate Federal regulator for any violation of this title that is alleged in that complaint.

(5) Limitations on state actions for violation of section 623(a)(1) [§ 1681s-2].

(A) Violation of injunction required. A State may not bring an action against a person under paragraph (1)(B) for a violation of section 623(a)(1) [§ 1681s-2], unless

(i) the person has been enjoined from committing the violation, in an action brought by the State under paragraph (1)(A); and

(ii) the person has violated the injunction.

(B) Limitation on damages recoverable. In an action against a person under paragraph (1)(B) for a violation of section 623(a)(1) [§ 1681s-2], a State may not recover any damages incurred before the date of the violation of an injunction on which the action is based.

(d) Enforcement under other authority. For the purpose of the exercise by any agency referred to in subsection (b) of this section of its powers under any Act referred to in that subsection, a violation of any requirement imposed under this title shall be deemed to be a violation of a requirement imposed under that Act. In addition to its powers under any provision of law specifically referred to in subsection (b) of this section, each of the agencies referred to in that subsection may exercise, for the purpose of enforcing compliance with any requirement imposed under this title any other authority conferred on it by law. Notwithstanding the preceding, no agency referred to in subsection (b) may conduct an examination of a bank, savings association, or credit union regarding compliance with the provisions of this title, except in response to a complaint (or if the agency otherwise has knowledge) that the bank, savings association, or credit union has violated a provision of this title, in which case, the agency may conduct an examination as necessary to investigate the complaint. If an agency determines during an investigation in response to a complaint that a violation of this title has occurred, the agency may, during its next 2 regularly scheduled examinations of the bank, savings association, or credit union, examine for compliance with this title.

(e) Interpretive authority. The Board of Governors of the Federal Reserve System may issue interpretations of any provision of this title as such provision may apply to any persons identified under paragraph (1), (2), and (3) of subsection (b), or to the holding companies and affiliates of such persons, in consultation with Federal agencies identified in paragraphs (1), (2), and (3) of subsection (b).

§ 622. Information on overdue child support obligations [15 U.S.C. §1681s-1]

Notwithstanding any other provision of this title, a consumer reporting agency shall include in any consumer report furnished by the agency in accordance with section 604 [§ 1681b] of this title, any information on the failure of the consumer to pay overdue support which

(1) is provided

(A) to the consumer reporting agency by a State or local child support enforcement agency; or

(B) to the consumer reporting agency and verified by any local, State, or Federal government agency; and

(2) antedates the report by 7 years or less.

§ 623. Responsibilities of furnishers of information to consumer reporting agencies [15 U.S.C. §1681s-2]

(a) Duty of furnishers of information to provide accurate information.

(1) Prohibition.

(A) Reporting information with actual knowledge of errors. A person shall not furnish any information relating to a consumer to any consumer reporting agency if the person knows or consciously avoids knowing that the information is inaccurate.

(B) Reporting information after notice and confirmation of errors. A person shall not furnish information relating to a consumer to any consumer reporting agency if

(i) the person has been notified by the consumer, at the address specified by the person for such notices, that specific information is inaccurate; and

(ii) the information is, in fact, inaccurate.

(C) No address requirement. A person who clearly and conspicuously specifies to the consumer an address for notices referred to in subparagraph (B) shall not be subject to subparagraph (A); however, nothing in subparagraph (B) shall require a person to specify such an address.

(2) Duty to correct and update information. A person who

(A) regularly and in the ordinary course of business furnishes information to one or more consumer reporting agencies about the person's transactions or experiences with any consumer; and

(B) has furnished to a consumer reporting agency information that the person determines is not complete or accurate,

shall promptly notify the consumer reporting agency of that determination and provide to the agency any corrections to that information, or any additional information, that is necessary to make the information provided by the person to the agency complete and accurate, and shall not thereafter furnish to the agency any of the information that remains not complete or accurate.

(3) Duty to provide notice of dispute. If the completeness or accuracy of any information furnished by any person to any consumer reporting agency is disputed to such person by a consumer, the person may not furnish the information to any consumer reporting agency without notice that such information is disputed by the consumer.

(4) Duty to provide notice of closed accounts. A person who regularly and in the ordinary course of business furnishes information to a consumer reporting agency regarding a consumer who has a credit account with that person shall notify the agency of the voluntary closure of the account by the consumer, in information regularly furnished for the period in which the account is closed.

(5) Duty to provide notice of delinquency of accounts. A person who furnishes information to a consumer reporting agency regarding a delinquent account being placed for collection, charged to profit or loss, or subjected to any similar action shall, not later than 90 days after furnishing the information, notify the agency of the month and year of the commencement of the delinquency that immediately preceded the action.

(b) Duties of furnishers of information upon notice of dispute.

(1) In general. After receiving notice pursuant to section 611(a)(2) [§ 1681i] of a dispute with regard to the completeness or accuracy of any information provided by a person to a consumer reporting agency, the person shall

(A) conduct an investigation with respect to the disputed information;

(B) review all relevant information provided by the consumer reporting agency pursuant to section 611(a)(2) [§ 1681i];

(C) report the results of the investigation to the consumer reporting agency; and

(D) if the investigation finds that the information is incomplete or inaccurate, report those results to all other consumer reporting agencies to which the person furnished the information and that compile and maintain files on consumers on a nationwide basis.

(2) Deadline. A person shall complete all investigations, reviews, and reports required under paragraph (1) regarding information provided by the person to a consumer reporting agency, before the expiration of the period under section 611(a)(1) [§ 1681i] within which the consumer reporting agency is required to complete actions required by that section regarding that information.

(c) Limitation on liability. Sections 616 and 617 [§§ 1681n and 1681o] do not apply to any failure to comply with subsection (a), except as provided in section 621(c)(1)(B) [§ 1681s].

(d) Limitation on enforcement. Subsection (a) shall be enforced exclusively under section 621 [§ 1681s] by the Federal agencies and officials and the State officials identified in that section.

§ 624. Relation to State laws [15 U.S.C. §1681t]

(a) In general. Except as provided in subsections (b) and (c), this title does not annul, alter, affect, or exempt any person subject to the provisions of this title from complying with the laws of any State with respect to the collection, distribution, or use of any information on consumers, except to the extent that those laws are inconsistent with any provision of this title, and then only to the extent of the inconsistency.

(b) General exceptions. No requirement or prohibition may be imposed under the laws of any State

(1) with respect to any subject matter regulated under

(A) subsection (c) or (e) of section 604 [§ 1681b], relating to the prescreening of consumer reports;

(B) section 611 [§ 1681i], relating to the time by which a consumer reporting agency must take any action, including the provision of notification to a consumer or other person, in any procedure related to the disputed accuracy of information in a consumer's file, except that this subparagraph shall not apply to any State law in effect on the date of enactment of the Consumer Credit Reporting Reform Act of 1996;

(C) subsections (a) and (b) of section 615 [§ 1681m], relating to the duties of a person who takes any adverse action with respect to a consumer;

(D) section 615(d) [§ 1681m], relating to the duties of persons who use a consumer report of a consumer in connection with any credit or insurance transaction that is not initiated by the consumer and that consists of a firm offer of credit or insurance;

(E) section 605 [§ 1681c], relating to information contained in consumer reports, except that this subparagraph shall not apply to any State law in effect on the date of enactment of the Consumer Credit Reporting Reform Act of 1996; or

(F) section 623 [§ 1681s-2], relating to the responsibilities of persons who furnish information to consumer reporting agencies,

except that this paragraph shall not apply
(i) with respect to section 54A(a) of chapter 93 of the Massachusetts Annotated Laws (as in effect on the date of enactment of the Consumer Credit Reporting Reform Act of 1996); or
(ii) with respect to section 1785.25(a) of the California Civil Code (as in effect on the date of enactment of the Consumer Credit Reporting Reform Act of 1996);

(2) with respect to the exchange of information among persons affiliated by common ownership or common corporate control, except that this paragraph shall not apply with respect to subsection (a) or (c)(1) of section 2480e of title 9, Vermont Statutes Annotated (as in effect on the date of enactment of the Consumer Credit Reporting Reform Act of 1996); or

(3) with respect to the form and content of any disclosure required to be made under section 609(c) [§ 1681g].

(c) Definition of firm offer of credit or insurance. Notwithstanding any definition of the term "firm offer of credit or insurance" (or any equivalent term) under the laws of any State, the definition of that term contained in section 603(l) [§ 1681a] shall be construed to apply in the enforcement and interpretation of the laws of any State governing consumer reports.

(d) Limitations. Subsections (b) and (c)

(1) do not affect any settlement, agreement, or consent judgment between any State Attorney General and any consumer reporting agency in effect on the date of enactment of the Consumer Credit Reporting Reform Act of 1996; and

(2) do not apply to any provision of State law (including any provision of a State constitution) that

(A) is enacted after January 1, 2004;
(B) states explicitly that the provision is intended to supplement this title; and
(C) gives greater protection to consumers than is provided under this title.

§ 625. Disclosures to FBI for counterintelligence purposes [15 U.S.C. §1681u]

(a) Identity of financial institutions. Notwithstanding section 604 [§ 1681b] or any other provision of this title, a consumer reporting agency shall furnish to the Federal Bureau of Investigation the names and addresses of all financial institutions (as that term is defined in section 1101 of the Right to Financial Privacy Act of 1978 [12 U.S.C. § 3401]) at which a consumer maintains or has maintained an account, to the extent that information is in the files of the agency, when presented with a written request for that information, signed by the Director of the Federal Bureau of Investigation, or the Director's designee, which certifies compliance with this section. The Director or the Director's designee may make such a certification only if the Director or the Director's designee has determined in writing that

(1) such information is necessary for the conduct of an authorized foreign counterintelligence investigation; and

(2) there are specific and articulable facts giving reason to believe that the consumer

(A) is a foreign power (as defined in section 101 of the Foreign Intelligence Surveillance Act of 1978 [50 U.S.C. § 1801]) or a person who is not a United States person (as defined in such section 101) and is an official of a foreign power; or

(B) is an agent of a foreign power and is engaging or has engaged in an act of international terrorism (as that term is defined in section 101(c) of the Foreign Intelligence Surveillance Act of 1978 [50 U.S.C. § 1801(c)]) or clandestine intelligence activities that involve or may involve a violation of criminal statutes of the United States.

(b) Identifying information. Notwithstanding the provisions of section 604 [§ 1681b] or any other provision of this title, a consumer reporting agency shall furnish identifying information respecting a consumer, limited to name, address, former addresses, places of employment, or former places of employment, to the Federal Bureau of Investigation when presented with a written request, signed by the Director or the Director's designee, which certifies compliance with this subsection. The Director or the Director's designee may make such a certification only if the Director or the Director's designee has determined in writing that

(1) such information is necessary to the conduct of an authorized counterintelligence investigation; and

(2) there is information giving reason to believe that the consumer has been, or is about to be, in contact with a foreign power or an agent of a foreign power (as defined in section 101 of the Foreign Intelligence Surveillance Act of 1978 [50 U.S.C. § 1801]).

(c) Court order for disclosure of consumer reports. Notwithstanding section 604 [§ 1681b] or any other provision of this title, if requested in writing by the Director of the Federal Bureau of Investigation, or a designee of the Director, a court may issue an order ex parte directing a consumer reporting agency to furnish a consumer report to the Federal Bureau of Investigation, upon a showing in camera that

(1) the consumer report is necessary for the conduct of an authorized foreign counterintelligence investigation; and

(2) there are specific and articulable facts giving reason to believe that the consumer whose consumer report is sought

(A) is an agent of a foreign power, and

(B) is engaging or has engaged in an act of international terrorism (as that term is defined in section 101(c) of the Foreign Intelligence Surveillance Act of 1978 [50 U.S.C. § 1801(c)]) or clandestine intelligence activities that involve or may involve a violation of criminal statutes of the United States.

The terms of an order issued under this subsection shall not disclose that the order is issued for purposes of a counterintelligence investigation.

(d) Confidentiality. No consumer reporting agency or officer, employee, or agent of a consumer reporting agency shall disclose to any person, other than those officers, employees, or agents of a consumer reporting agency necessary to fulfill the requirement to disclose information to the Federal Bureau of Investigation under this section, that the Federal Bureau of Investigation has sought or obtained the identity of financial institutions or a consumer report respecting any consumer under subsection (a), (b), or (c), and no consumer reporting agency or officer, employee, or agent of a consumer reporting agency shall include in any consumer report any information that would indicate that the Federal Bureau of Investigation has sought or obtained such information or a consumer report.

(e) Payment of fees. The Federal Bureau of Investigation shall, subject to the availability of appropriations, pay to the consumer reporting agency assembling or providing report or information in accordance with procedures established under this section a fee for reimbursement for such costs as are reasonably necessary and which have been directly incurred in searching, reproducing, or transporting books, papers, records, or other data required or requested to be produced under this section.

(f) Limit on dissemination. The Federal Bureau of Investigation may not disseminate information obtained pursuant to this section outside of the Federal Bureau of Investigation, except to other Federal agencies as may be necessary for the approval or conduct of a foreign counterintelligence investigation, or, where the information concerns a person subject to the Uniform Code of Military Justice, to appropriate investigative authorities within the military department concerned as may be necessary for the conduct of a joint foreign counterintelligence investigation.

(g) Rules of construction. Nothing in this section shall be construed to prohibit information from being furnished by the Federal Bureau of Investigation pursuant to a subpoena or court order, in connection with a judicial or administrative proceeding to enforce the provisions of this Act. Nothing in this section shall be construed to authorize or permit the withholding of information from the Congress.

(h) Reports to Congress. On a semiannual basis, the Attorney General shall fully inform the Permanent Select Committee on Intelligence and the Committee on Banking, Finance and Urban Affairs of the House of Representatives, and the Select Committee on Intelligence and the Committee on Banking, Housing, and Urban Affairs of the Senate concerning all requests made pursuant to subsections (a), (b), and (c).

(i) Damages. Any agency or department of the United States obtaining or disclosing any consumer reports, records, or information contained therein in violation of this section is liable to the consumer to whom such consumer reports, records, or information relate in an amount equal to the sum of

(1) $100, without regard to the volume of consumer reports, records, or information involved;

(2) any actual damages sustained by the consumer as a result of the disclosure;

(3) if the violation is found to have been willful or intentional, such punitive damages as a court may allow; and

(4) in the case of any successful action to enforce liability under this subsection, the costs of the action, together with reasonable attorney fees, as determined by the court.

(j) Disciplinary actions for violations. If a court determines that any agency or department of the United States has violated any provision of this section and the court finds that the circumstances surrounding the violation raise questions of whether or not an officer or employee of the agency or department acted willfully or intentionally with respect to the violation, the agency or department shall promptly initiate a proceeding to determine whether or not disciplinary action is warranted against the officer or employee who was responsible for the violation.

(k) Good-faith exception. Notwithstanding any other provision of this title, any consumer reporting agency or agent or employee thereof making disclosure of consumer reports or identifying information pursuant to this subsection in good-faith reliance upon a certification of the Federal Bureau of Investigation pursuant to provisions of this section shall not be liable to any person for such disclosure under this title, the constitution of any State, or any law or regulation of any State or any political subdivision of any State.

(l) Limitation of remedies. Notwithstanding any other provision of this title, the remedies and sanctions set forth in this section shall be the only judicial remedies and sanctions for violation of this section.

(m) Injunctive relief. In addition to any other remedy contained in this section, injunctive relief shall be available to require compliance with the procedures of this section. In the event of any successful action under this subsection, costs together with reasonable attorney fees, as determined by the court, may be recovered.

Legislative History

- ❑ House Reports: No. 91-975 (Comm. on Banking and Currency) and No. 91-1587 (Comm. of Conference)

- ❑ Senate Reports: No. 91-1139 accompanying S. 3678 (Comm. on Banking and Currency)
- ❑ Congressional Record, Vol. 116 (1970)
- ❑ May 25, considered and passed House.
- ❑ Sept. 18, considered and passed Senate, amended.
- ❑ Oct. 9, Senate agreed to conference report.
- ❑ Oct. 13, House agreed to conference report.

Enactment:

- ❑ Public Law No. 91-508 (October 26, 1970):

Amendments: Public Law Nos.

- ❑ 95-473 (October 17, 1978)
- ❑ 95-598 (November 6, 1978)
- ❑ 98-443 (October 4, 1984)
- ❑ 101-73 (August 9, 1989)
- ❑ 102-242 (December 19, 1991)
- ❑ 102-537 (October 27, 1992)
- ❑ 102-550 (October 28, 1992)
- ❑ 103-325 (September 23, 1994)
- ❑ 104-88 (December 29, 1995)
- ❑ 104-93 (January 6, 1996)
- ❑ 104-193 (August 22, 1996)
- ❑ 104-208 (September 30, 1996)
- ❑ 105-107 (November 20, 1997)
- ❑ 105-347 (November 2, 1998)

Notes

1. The reporting periods have been lengthened for certain adverse information pertaining to U.S. Government insured or guaranteed student loans, or pertaining to national direct student loans. See sections 430A(f) and 463(c)(3) of the Higher Education Act of 1965, 20 U.S.C. 1080a(f) and 20 U.S.C. 1087cc(c)(3), respectively.
2. Should read "paragraphs (4) and (5) ..." Prior Section 605(a)(6) was amended and redesignated as Section 605(a)(5) in November 1998.

Appendix B

The Equal Credit Opportunity Act 15 U.S.C. 1691-1691c

701 Prohibited Discrimination: Reasons for Adverse Action

(a) It shall be unlawful for any creditor to discriminate against any applicant, with respect to any aspect of a credit transaction—

> (1) on the basis of race, color, religion, national origin, sex or marital status, or age (provided the applicant has the capacity to contract):
>
> (2) because all or part of the applicant's income derives from any public assistance program; or
>
> (3) because the applicant has in good faith exercised any right under the Consumer Credit Protection Act.

(b) It shall not constitute discrimination for purposes of this title for a creditor—

> (1) to make an inquiry of marital status if such inquiry is for the purpose of ascertaining the creditor rights and remedies applicable to the particular extension of credit and not to discriminate in a determination of creditworthiness;

(2) to make an inquiry of the applicant's age or whether the applicant's income derives from any public assistance program if such inquiry is for the purpose of determining the amount and probable continuance of income levels, credit history, or other pertinent element of creditworthiness as provided in regulations of the Board:

(3) to use any empirically derived credit system which considers age if such system is demonstrably and statistically sound in accordance with regulations of the Board, except that in the operation of such system the age of an elderly applicant may not be assigned a negative factor or value; or

(4) to make an inquiry or to consider the age of an elderly applicant when the age of such applicant is to be used by the creditor in the extension of credit in favor of such applicant.

(c) It is not a violation of this section for a creditor to refuse to extend credit offered pursuant to—

(1) any credit assistance program expressly authorized by law for an economically disadvantaged class of persons;

(2) any credit assistance program administered by a nonprofit organization for its members or an economically disadvantaged class of persons; or

(3) any special purpose credit program offered by a profit-making organization to meet special social needs, which meets standards prescribed in regulations by the Board; if such refusal is required by or made pursuant to such program.

(d) Reason for adverse action, procedure applicable; "adverse action" defined—

(1) Within thirty days (or such longer reasonable time as specified in regulations of the Board for any class of credit transaction) after receipt of a completed application for credit, a creditor shall notify the applicant of its action on the application.

(2) Each applicant against whom adverse action is taken shall be entitled to a statement of reasons for such action from the creditor. A creditor satisfies this obligation by —

(A) providing statements of reasons in writing as a matter of course to applicants against whom adverse action is taken; or

(B) giving written notification of adverse action which discloses

(i) the applicant's right to a statement of reasons within thirty days after receipt by the creditor of a request made within sixty days after such notification, and

(ii) the identity of the person or office from which such statement may be obtained. Such statement may be given orally if the written notification advises the applicant of his right to have the statement of reasons confirmed in writing on written request.

(3) A statement of reasons meets the requirements of this section only if it contains the specific reasons for the adverse action taken.

(4) Where a creditor has been requested by a third party to make a specific extension of credit directly or indirectly to an applicant, the notification and statement of reasons required by this subsection may be made directly by such creditor, or indirectly through the third party, provided in either case that the identity of the creditor is disclosed.

(5) The requirements of paragraph (2), (3), or (4) may be satisfied by verbal statements or notification in the case of any creditor who did not act on more than 150 applications during the calendar year preceding the calendar year in which the adverse action is taken, as determined under regulations of the Board.

(6) For purposes of this subsection, the term "adverse action" means a denial or revocation of credit, a change in the terms of an existing credit arrangement, or a refusal to grant credit in substantially the amount or on substantially the terms requested. Such term does not include a refusal to extend additional credit under an existing credit arrangement where the applicant is delinquent or otherwise in default, or where such additional credit would exceed a previously established credit limit. (Amended by Act of 3/23/76, P.L. 94-239, eff. 3/23/77.)

702 Definitions

(a) The definition and rules of construction set forth in the section are applicable for the purpose of this title.
(b) The term "applicant" means any person who applies to a creditor directly for an extension, renewal, or continuation of credit, or applies to a creditor, indirectly by use of an existing credit plan for an amount exceeding a previously established credit limit.
(c) The term "Board" refers to the Board of Governors of the Federal Reserve System.
(d) The term "credit" means the right granted by a creditor to a debtor to defer payment of debt or to incur debts and defer its payment or to purchase property or services and defer payment therefore.
(e) The term "creditor" means any person who regularly extends, renews, or continues credit; any person who regularly arranges for the extension, renewal, or continuation of credit; or any assignee of an original creditor who participates in the decision to extend, renew, or continue credit.
(f) The term "person" means a natural person, a corporation, government or governmental subdivision or agency, trust, estate, partnership, cooperative, or association.
(g) Any reference to any requirement imposed under this title or any provision thereof includes reference to the regulations of the Board under this title or the provision thereof in question.

703 Regulations

(a) The Board shall prescribe regulations to carry out the purposes of this title. These regulations may contain but are not limited to such classifications, differentiations, or other provision, and may provide for such adjustments and exceptions for any class of transactions, as in the judgment of the Board are necessary or proper to effectuate the purposes of this title, to prevent circumvention or evasion thereof, or to facilitate or substantiate compliance therewith. Such regulations shall be prescribed as soon as possible after the date of enactment of this Act, but in no event later than the effective date of this Act. In particular, such regulations may exempt from one or more of the previsions of this title any class of transactions not primarily for personal, family, or household purposes, if the Board makes an express finding that the application of such provision or provisions would not contribute substantially to carrying out the purposes of this title.

(b) The Board shall establish a Consumer Advisory Council to advise and consult with it in the exercise of its functions under the Consumer Credit Protection Act and to advise and consult with it concerning other consumer related matters it may place before the council. In appointing the members of the Council, the Board shall seek to achieve a fair representation of the interests of creditors and consumers. The Council shall meet from time to time at the call of the Board. Members of the Council who are not regular full-time employees of the United States shall, while attending meetings of such Council, be entitled to receive compensation at a rate fixed by the Board, but not exceeding $100 per day, including travel time. Such members may be allowed travel expenses, including transportation and subsistence, while away from their homes or regular place of business. (Amended by Act of 3-23-76, P.L. 94-239 eff. 3-23-76.)

704 Administrative Enforcement

(a) Compliance with the requirements imposed under this title shall be enforced under:

(1) Section 8 of the Federal Deposit Insurance Act, in the case of—

(A) national banks, by the Comptroller of the Currency,

(B) member banks of the Federal Reserve System (other than national banks), by the Board,

(C) banks insured by the Federal Deposit Insurance Corporation (other than members of the Federal Reserve System), by the Board of Directors of the Federal Deposit Insurance Corporation.

(2) Section 5(d) of the Home Owners Loan Act of 1933, section 407 of the National Housing Act, and sections 6(i) and 17 of the Federal Home Loan Bank Act, by the Federal Home Loan Bank Board (acting directly or through the Federal Savings and Loan Insurance Corporation), in the case of any institution subject to any of those provisions.

(3) The Federal Credit Union Act, by the Administrator of the National Credit Union Administration with respect to any Federal Credit Union.

(4) The Acts to regulate commerce by the Interstate Commerce Commission with respect to any common carrier subject to those Acts.
(5) The Federal Aviation Act of 1958, by the Civil Aeronautics Board with respect to any air carrier or foreign air carrier subject to that Act.
(6) The Packers and Stockyards Act of 1921 (except as provided in section 406 of the Act), by the Secretary of Agriculture with respect to any activities subject to that act.
(7) The Farm Credit Act of 1971, by the Farm Credit Administration with respect to any Federal land bank, Federal land bank association, Federal intermediate credit bank, and production credit association;
(8) The Securities Exchange Act of 1934, by the Securities and Exchange Commission with respect to brokers and dealers; and
(9) The Small Business Investment Act of 1958, by the Small Business Administration, with respect to small business investment companies.

(b) For the purpose of the exercise by an agency referred to in subsection (a) of its power under any Act referred to in that subsection, a violation of any requirement imposed under this title shall be deemed to be a violation of a requirement imposed under that Act. In addition to its powers under any provision of law specifically referred to in subsection (a), each of the agencies referred to in that subsection may exercise for the purpose of enforcing compliance with any requirement imposed under this title, any other authority conferred on it by law. The exercise of the authorities of any of the agencies referred to in subsection (a) for the purpose of enforcing compliance with any requirement imposed under this title shall in no way preclude the exercise of such authorities for the purpose of enforcing compliance with any other provision of law not relating to the prohibition of discrimination on the basis of sex or marital status with respect to any aspect of a credit transaction.

705 Relation to State Laws

(a) A request for the signature of both parties to a marriage for the purpose of creating a valid lien, passing clear title, waiving inchoate rights to a property, or assigning earnings, shall not constitute discrimination under this title: provided, however, that this provision shall not be construed to permit a creditor to take sex or marital status into account in connection with the evaluation of creditworthiness of any applicant.

(b) Consideration or application of State property laws directly or indirectly affecting creditworthiness shall not constitute discrimination for purposes of this title.

(c) Any provision of State law which prohibits the separate extension of consumer credit to each party to a marriage shall not apply in any case where each party to a marriage voluntarily applies for a separate credit from the same creditor: provided, that in any case where such a State law is so preempted, each party to the marriage shall be solely responsible for the debt so contracted.

(d) When each party to a marriage separately and voluntarily applies for and obtains separate credit accounts with the same creditor, these accounts shall not be aggregated or otherwise combined for purposes of determining permissible finance charges or permissible loan ceilings under the laws of any State or of the United States.

(e) Where the same act or omission constitutes a violation of this title and of applicable State law, a person aggrieved by such State law, but not both. This election of remedies shall not apply to court actions in which the relief sought does not include monetary damages or to administrative actions.

(f) This title does not annul, alter or affect, or exempt any person subject to the provisions of this title from complying with the laws of any State with respect to credit discrimination, except to the extent that those laws are inconsistent with any prevision of this title, and then only to the extent of the inconsistency. The Board is authorized to determine whether such inconsistencies exist. The Board may not determine that any State law is inconsistent with any prevision of this title if the Board determines that such law gives greater protection to the applicant.

(g) The Board shall be regulation exempt from the requirements of sections 701 and 702 of this title any class of credit transactions within any State if it determines that under the law of that State that class of transactions is subject to requirements substantially similar to those imposed under this title or that such law gives greater protection to the applicant and that there is adequate prevision for enforcement. Failure to comply with any requirement of such State law in any transaction so exempted shall constitute a violation of this title for the purposes of section 706. (Amended by Act of 3 -23-76, P.L. 94-239, eff. 3-23-76.)

706 Civil Liability

(a) Any creditor who fails to comply with any requirement imposed under this title shall be liable to the aggrieved applicant for any actual damages sustained by such applicant acting either in an individual capacity or as a member of a class.

(b) Any creditor, other than a government or governmental subdivision or agency, who fails to comply with any requirement imposed under this title shall be liable to the aggrieved applicant for punitive damages in an amount not greater than $10,000, in addition to any actual damages provided in subsection (a), except that in the case of a class action the total recovery under this subsection shall not exceed the lesser or $500,000 or 1 per centum of the net worth of the creditor. In determining the amount of such damages in any action, the court shall consider, among other relevant factors, the amount of any actual damages awarded, the frequency and persistence of failures of compliance by the creditor, the resources of the creditor, the number of persons adversely affected, and the extent to which the creditor's failure of compliance was intentional.

(c) Upon application by an aggrieved applicant, the appropriate United States district court or any other court of competent jurisdiction may grant such equitable and declaratory relief as is necessary to enforce the requirements imposed under this title.

(d) In the case of any successful action under subsection (a), (b), or (c), the costs of the action, together with a reasonable attorney's fee as determined by the court, shall be added to any damages awarded by the court under such subsection.

(e) No provision of this title imposing liability shall apply to any act done or omitted in good faith in conformity with any official rule, regulation, or interpretation thereof by the Board or in conformity with any interpretation or approval by an official or employee of the Federal Reserve System duly authorized by the Board to issue such interpretations or approvals under such procedures as the Board may prescribe therefore, notwithstanding that after such act or omission has occurred, such rule, regulation, interpretation, or approval is amended, rescinded, or determined by judicial or other authority to be invalid for any reason.

(f) Any action under this section may be brought in the appropriate United States district court without regard to the amount in controversy, or in any other court of competent jurisdiction. No such action shall be brought later than two years from the date of the occurrence of the violation, except—

(1) whenever any agency having responsibility for administrative enforcement under section 704 commences an enforcement proceeding within two years from the date of the occurrence of the violation.

(2) whenever the Attorney General commences a civil action under this section within two years from the date of occurrence of the violation, then any applicant who has been a victim of the discrimination which is the subject of such proceeding or civil action may bring an action under this section not later than one year after the commencement of that proceeding or action.

(g) The agencies having responsibility for administrative enforcement under section 704, if unable to obtain compliance with section 701, are authorized to refer the matter to the Attorney General with a recommendation that an appropriate civil action be instituted.

(h) When a matter is referred to the Attorney General pursuant to subsection (g), or whenever he has reason to believe that one or more creditors are engaged in a pattern or practice in violation of this title, the Attorney General may bring a civil action in any appropriate United States district court far such relief as may be appropriate, including injunctive relief.

(i) No person aggrieved by a violation of this title and by a violation of section 805 of the Civil Rights Act of 1968 shall recover under this title and section 812 of the Civil Rights Act of 1968, if such violation is based on the same transaction.

(j) Nothing in this title shall be construed to prohibit the discovery of a creditor's granting standards under appropriate discovery procedures in the court agency in which an action or proceeding is brought. (Amended by Act of 3-23-76, P.L. 94-239, eff. 3-23-76.)

707 Annual Reports to Congress

Annual reports to Congress—Not later than February 1 of each year after 1976, the Board and the Attorney General shall, respectively, make reports to the Congress concerning the administration of their functions under this title, including such recommendations as the Board and the Attorney General, respectively, deem necessary or appropriate. In addition, each report of the Board shall include its assessment of the extent to which compliance with the requirements of this title is being achieved, and a summary of the enforcement actions taken by each of the agencies assigned administrative enforcement responsibilities under section 704. (Amended by Act of 3-23-76, P.L. 94-239, eff. 2-23-76.)

708 Effective Date

This title takes effect upon the expiration of one year after the date of its enactment. The amendments made by the Equal Credit Opportunity Act Amendments of 1976 shall take effect on the date of enactment thereof and shall apply to any violation occurring on or after such date, except that the amendment made to section 701 of the Equal Credit Opportunity Act shall take effect 12 months after the date of enactment. (Amended by Act of 3-23-76, P.L. 94-239, eff. 3-23-76.)

709 Short Title

This title may be cited as the Equal Credit Opportunity Act.

Regulation B: Part 202 Equal Credit Opportunity Act (12CFR, Part 202, Fed. Reg. 48018)

Sections

202.1 Authority, scope, and purpose
202.2 Definitions
202.3 Limited exceptions for certain classes of transactions
202.4 General rule prohibiting discrimination
202.5 Rules concerning taking of applications
202.6 Rules concerning evaluation of applications
202.7 Rules concerning extensions of credit
202.8 Special purpose credit programs
202.9 Notifications
202.10 Furnishing of credit information
202.11 Relation to state law
202.12 Record retention

202.1 Authority, scope, and purpose

(a) Authority and Scope. This regulation is issued by the Board of Governors of the Federal Reserve System pursuant to title VII (Equal Credit Opportunity Act) of the Consumer Credit Protection Act, as amended (15 USC 1601 et seq.). Except as otherwise provided herein, the regulation applies to all persons who are creditors, as defined in 202.2(1). Information collection requirements contained in this regulation have been approved by the Office of Management and Budget under the previsions of 44 USC 3501 et seq. and have been assigned OMB No. 7100-0201.
(b) Purpose. The purpose of this regulation is to promote the availability of credit to all creditworthy applicants without regard to race, color, religion, national origin, sex, marital status, or age (provided the applicant has the capacity to contract); to the fact that all or part of the applicant's income derives from a public assistance program; or to the fact that the applicant has in good faith exercised any right under the Consumer Credit Protection Act. The regulation prohibits creditor practices that discriminate on the basis of any of these factors. The regulation also required creditors to notify applicants of action taken on their applications; to report credit history in the names of both spouses on an account; to retain records of credit applications; and to collect information about the applicant's race and other personal characteristics in applications for certain dwelling-related loans.

202.2 Definitions

For the purposes of this regulation, unless the context indicates otherwise, the following definitions apply.
(a) Account means an extension of credit. When employed in relation to an account, the word use refers only to an open-end credit.
(b) Act means the Equal Credit Opportunity Act (title VII of the Consumer Credit Protection Act).
(c) Adverse Action.

(1) The term means:

(i) A refusal to grant credit in substantially the amount or on substantially the terms requested in an application unless the creditor makes a counteroffer (to grant credit in a different amount or on other terms) and the applicant uses or expressly accepts the credit offered;

(ii) A termination of an account or an unfavorable change in the terms of an account that does not affect all or a substantial portion of a class of the creditor's accounts; or

(iii) A refusal to increase the amount of credit available to an applicant who has made an application for an increase.

(2) The term does not include:

(i) A change in the terms of an account expressly agreed to by an applicant;

(ii) Any action or forbearance relating to an account taken in connection with inactivity, default, or delinquency as to that account;

(iii) A refusal or failure to authorize an account transaction at a point of sale, or loan, except when the refusal is a termination or an unfavorable change in the terms of an account that does not affect all or a substantial portion of a class of the creditor's accounts, or when the refusal is a denial of an application for an increase in the amount of credit available under the account;

(iv) A refusal to extend credit because applicable law prohibits the credit from extending the credit request; or

(v) A refusal to extend credit because the creditor does not offer the type of credit or credit plan requested.

(3) An action that falls within the definition of both paragraphs (c) (1) and (c) (2) of this section is governed by paragraph (c) (2).

(d) Age refers only to the age of natural persons and means the number of fully elapsed years from the date of an applicant's birth.
(e) Applicant means any person who requests or who has received an extension of credit from a creditor, and includes any person who is or may become contractually liable regarding an extension of credit. For purposes of 202.7(d), the term includes guarantors, sureties, endorsers, and similar parties.
(f) Application means an oral or written request for an extension of credit that is made in accordance with procedures established by a creditor for the type of credit requested. The term does not include the use of an account or line of credit to obtain an amount of credit that is within a previously established credit limit. A completed application means an application in connection with which a creditor has received all the information that the creditor regularly obtains and considers in evaluating applications for the amount and type of credit requested from the applicant, and any additional information requested from the applicant, and any approvals or reports by governmental agencies or other persons that are necessary to guarantee, insure, or provide security for the credit or collateral. The creditor shall exercise reasonable diligence in obtaining such information.
(g) Board means the Board of Governors of the Federal Reserve System.
(h) Consumer credit means extended to a natural person primarily for personal, family, or household purposes.
(i) Contractually liable means expressly obligated to repay all debts arising on an account by reason of an agreement to that effect.
(j) Credit means the right granted by a creditor to an applicant to defer payment of a debt, incur debt and defer its payment, or purchase property or services and defer payment thereof.
(k) Credit card means any card, plate, coupon book, or other single credit device that may be used from time to time to obtain money, property, or services on credit.
(l) Creditor means a person who, in the ordinary course of business, regularly participates in the decision of whether or not to extend credit. The term includes a creditor's assignee, transferee, or subrogee who so participates. For purposes of 202.4 and 202.5(a), the term also includes a person who, in the ordinary course of business, regularly refers applicants or prospective applicants to creditors, or selects or offers to select creditors to whom requests for credit may be made. A person is not a creditor regarding any violation of the act or this regulation committed by another creditor unless the person

knew or had reasonable notice of the act, policy, or practice that constituted the violation before becoming involved in the credit transaction. The term does not include a person whose only participation in a credit transaction involves honoring a credit card.

(m) Credit transaction means every aspect of an applicants dealings with a creditor regarding an application for credit or an existing extension of credit (including, but not limited to, information requirements; investigation procedures; standards of creditworthiness; terms of credit; furnishing of credit information; revocation, alteration, or termination of credit; and collection procedures).

(n) Discriminate against an applicant means to treat an applicant less favorably than other applicants.

(o) Elderly means age 62 or older.

(p) Empirically derived and other credit scoring systems.

(1) A credit scoring system is a system that evaluates an applicant's creditworthiness mechanically, based on key attributes of the applicant and aspects of the transaction, and that determines, alone or in conjunction with an evaluation of additional information about the applicant, whether an applicant is deemed creditworthy. To qualify as an empirically derived, demonstrably and statistically sound credit scoring system, the system must be:

(i) Based on data that are derived from an empirical comparison of sample groups or the population of creditworthy and noncreditworthy applicants who apply for credit within a reasonable preceding period of time;

(ii) Developed for the purpose of evaluating the creditworthiness of applicants with respect to the legitimate business interests of the creditor utilizing the system (including, but not limited to, minimizing bad debt losses and operating expenses in accordance with the creditor's business judgment);

(iv) Developed and validated using accepted statistical principles and methodology and adjusted as necessary to maintain predictive ability.

(2) A creditor may use an empirically derived, demonstrably and statistically sound credit scoring system obtained from another person or may obtain credit experience from which to develop such a system. Any such system must satisfy the criteria set forth in paragraph (p)(1)(i) through (iv) of this section; if the creditor is unable during the development process to validate the system based on its own credit experience in accordance with paragraph (p)(1) of this section, the system must be validated when sufficient credit experience becomes available. A system that fails this validity test is no longer an empirically derived, demonstrably and statistically sound credit scoring system for that creditor.

(q) Extend credit and extension for credit mean the granting of credit in any form (including, but not limited to, credit granted in addition to any existing credit or credit limit; credit granted pursuant to an open-end credit plan; the refinancing or other renewal of credit; including the issuance of a new credit card in place of an expiring credit card or in substitution for an existing credit card; the consolidation of two or more obligations; or the continuance of existing credit without any special effort to collect at or after maturity).

(r) Good faith means honesty in fact in the conduct or transaction.

(s) Inadvertent error means a mechanical, electronic, or clerical error that a creditor demonstrates was not intentional and occurred notwithstanding the maintenance of procedures reasonably adapted to avoid such errors.

(t) Judgmental system of evaluating applicants means any system for evaluating the creditworthiness of an applicant other than an empirically derived, demonstrably and statistically sound credit scoring system.

(u) Marital status means the state of being unmarried, married, or separated, as defined by applicable state law. The term "unmarried" includes persons who are single, divorced, or widowed.

(v) Negative factor or value, in relation to the age of elderly applicants, means utilizing a factor, value, or weight that is less favorable regarding elderly applicants than the creditor's experience warrants or is less favorable than the factor, value, or weight assigned to the class of applicants that are not classified as elderly and are most favored by a creditor on the basis of age.

(w) Open-end credit means credit extended under a plan by which a creditor may permit an applicant to make purchases or obtain loans from time to time directly from the creditor or indirectly by use of a credit card, check, or other device.

(x) Person means a natural person, corporation, government or governmental subdivision or agency, trust, estate, partnership, cooperative, or association.

(y) Pertinent element of creditworthiness, in relation to a judgmental system of evaluating applicants, means any information about applicants that a creditor obtains and considers and that has a demonstrable relationship to a determination of creditworthiness.

(z) Prohibited basis means race, color, religion, national origin, sex, marital status, or age (provided that the applicant has the capacity to enter into a binding contract); the fact that all or part of the applicant's income derives from any public assistance program; or the fact that the applicant has in good faith exercised any right under the Consumer Credit Protection Act or any state law upon which an exemption has been granted by the Board.

(aa) State means any State, the District of Columbia, the Commonwealth of Puerto Rico or any territory or possession of the United States.

202.3 Limited exceptions for certain classes of transactions

(a) Public utilities credit.

(1) Definition. Public utilities credit refers to extensions of credit that involve public utility services provided through pipe, wire, or other connected facilities, or radio or similar transmissions (including extensions of such facilities), if the charges for service, delayed payment, and any discount for prompt payment are filed with or regulated by a government unit.

(2) Exceptions. The following provisions of this regulation do not apply to public utilities credit:

(i) Section 202.5 (d)(1) concerning information about marital status;

(ii) Section 202.10 relating to furnishing of credit information; and

(iii) Section 202.12(b) relating to record retention.

(b) Securities credit—

(l) Definition. Securities credit refers to extensions of credit subject to regulation under section 7 of the Securities Exchange Act of 1934 or extensions of credit by a broker or dealer subject to regulation as a broker or dealer under the Securities Exchange Act of 1934

(2) Exceptions. The following provisions of this regulation do not apply to securities credit:

(i) Section 202.5(c) concerning information about a spouse or former spouse;

(ii) Section 202.5(d)(1) concerning information about marital status;

(iii) Section 202.5(d)(3) concerning information about the sex of an applicant;

(iv) Section 202.7(b) relation to designation of name, but only to the extent necessary to prevent violation or rules regarding an account in which a broker or dealer has an interest, or rules necessitating the aggregation of accounts of spouses for the purpose of determining controlling interests, beneficial interests, beneficial ownership, or purchase limitations and restrictions;

(v) Section 202.7(c) relating to action concerning open-end accounts, but only to the extent the action taken is on the basis of a change of name or marital status;

(vi) Section 202.7(d) relating to the signature of a spouse or other person;

(vii) Section 202.10 relating to furnishing of credit information; and

(viii) Section 202.12(b) relating to record retention.

(c) Incidental credit.

(1) Definition. Incidental credit refers to extensions of consumer credit other than credit of the types described in paragraphs (1) and (b) of this section:

(i) That are not made pursuant to the terms of a credit card account:

(ii) That are not subject to a finance charge (as defined in Regulation Z, 12CFR 226.4); and that are not payable by agreement in more than four installments.

(2) Exceptions. The following provisions of this regulation do not apply to incidental credit;

(i) Section 202.5(c) concerning information about a spouse or former spouse;

(ii) Section 202.5(d)(1) concerning information about marital status;

(iii) Section 202.5(d)(2) concerning information about income derived from alimony, child support, or separate maintenance payments;

(iv) Section 202.5(d)(3) concerning information about the sex of an applicant, but only to the extent necessary for medical records or similar purposes;

(v) Section 202.7(d) relating to the signature of a spouse or other person;

(vi) Section 202.9 relating to notifications;

(vii) Section 202.10 relating to furnishing of credit information; and

(viii) Section 202.12(b) relation to record retention.

(d) Business credit.

(1) Definition. Business credit refers to extensions of credit primarily for business or commercial (including agricultural) purposes, but excluding extensions of credit of the types described in paragraphs (a) and (b) of this section.

(2) Exceptions. The following provisions of this regulation do not apply to business credit:

(i) Section 202.5(d)(1) concerning information about marital status; and

(ii) Section 202.10 relating to furnishing of credit information.

(3) Modified requirements. The following provisions of this regulation apply to business credit as specified below:

(i) Section 202.9 (a), (b), and (c) relating to notifications; the creditor shall notify the applicant, orally or in writing, of action taken of incompleteness. When credit is denied or when other adverse action is taken, the creditor is required to provide a written statement of the reasons and the ECOA notice specified in section 202.9(b) if the applicant makes a written request for the reasons within 30 days of that notification; and

(ii) Section 202.12(b) relating to record retention; the creditor shall retain records as provided in 202.12(b) if the applicant, within 90 days after being notified of action taken or of incompleteness, requests in writing that records be retained.

(e) Government credit.

(1) Definition. Government credit refers to extensions of credit made to governments or governmental subdivisions, agencies, or instrumentalities.

(2) Applicability of regulation. Except for section 202.4 the general rule prohibiting discrimination of a prohibited basis, the requirements of this regulation do not apply to government credit.

202.4 General rule prohibiting discrimination

A creditor shall not discriminate against an applicant on a prohibited basis regarding any aspect of a credit transaction.

202.5 Rules concerning taking of applications

(a) Discouraging applications. A creditor shall not make any oral or written statement, in advertising or otherwise, to applicants or prospective applicants that would discourage on a prohibited basis a reasonable person from making or pursuing an application.

(b) General rules concerning requests for information.

(1) Except as provided in paragraphs (c) and (d) of this section, a creditor may request any information in connection with an application.

(2) Required collection of information. Notwithstanding paragraphs (c) and (d) of this section, a creditor shall request information for monitoring purposes as required by 202.13 for credit secured by the applicant's dwelling. In addition, a creditor may obtain information required by a regulation, order, or agreement issued by, or entered into with, a court or an enforcement agency (including the Attorney General of the United States or a similar state official) to monitor or enforce compliance with the act, this regulation, or other federal or state statute or regulation.

(3) Specified purpose credit. A creditor may obtain information that is otherwise restricted to determine eligibility for a special purpose credit program, as provided in 202.8(c) and (d).

(c) Information about a spouse or former spouse.

(1) Except as permitted in this paragraph, a creditor may not request any information concerning the spouse or former spouse of an applicant.

(2) Permissible inquiries. A creditor may request any information concerning an applicant's spouse (or former spouse) under paragraph (c)(2)(v) that may be requested about the applicant if—

(i) The spouse will be permitted to use the account;

(ii) The spouse will be contractually liable on the account;

(iii) The applicant is relying on the spouse's income as a basis for repayment of the credit requested;

(iv) The applicant resides in a community property state or property on which the applicant is relying as a basis for repayment of

the credit requested is located in such a state;
or
(v) The applicant is relying on alimony, child support, or separate maintenance payments from a spouse or former spouse as basis for repayment of the credit requested.

(3) Other accounts of the applicant. A creditor may request an applicant to list any account upon which the applicant is liable and to provide the name and address in which the account is carried. A creditor may also ask the names in which an applicant has previously received credit.

(d) Other limitations on information requests.

(1) Marital status. If an applicant applies for individual unsecured credit, a creditor shall not inquire about the applicant's marital status unless the applicant resides in a community property state or is relying on property located in such a state as a basis for repayment of the credit requested. If an application is for other than individual unsecured credit, a creditor may inquire about the applicant's marital status, but shall use only the terms "married," "unmarried," and "separated." A creditor may explain that the category "unmarried" includes single, divorced, and widowed persons.

(2) Disclosure about income from alimony, child support, or separate maintenance. A creditor shall not inquire whether income stated in an application is derived from alimony, child support, or separate maintenance payments unless the creditor discloses to the applicant that such income need not be revealed if the applicant does not want the creditor to consider it in determining the applicants creditworthiness.

(3) Sex. A creditor shall not inquire about the sex of an applicant. An applicant may be requested to designate a title on an application form (such as Ms. Miss, Mr., or Mrs.) if the form discloses that the designation of a title is optional. An applicant form shall otherwise use only terms that are neutral as to sex.

(4) Childbearing, child-rearing. A creditor shall not inquire about birth control practices, intentions concerning the bearing or rearing of children, or capability to bear children.

A creditor may inquire about the number and ages of an applicant's dependents or about dependent-related financial obligations or expenditures, provided such information is requested without regard to sex, marital status, or any other prohibited basis.

(5) Race, color, religion, national origins. A creditor shall not inquire about the race, color, religion, or national origin of an applicant or any other person in connection with a credit transaction. A creditor may inquire about an applicant's permanent residence and immigration status.

(e) Written applications. A creditor shall take written applications for the types of credit covered by 202.13 (a), but need not take written applications for other types of credit.

202.6 Rules concerning evaluation of applications

(a) General rule concerning use of information. Except as otherwise provided in the act and this regulation, a creditor may consider information obtained, so long as the information is not used to discriminate against an applicant on a prohibited basis.

(b) Specific rules concerning use of information.

(1) Except as provided in the act and this regulation, a creditor shall not take a prohibited basis into account in any system of evaluating the creditworthiness of applicants.

(2) Age, receipt of public assistance.

(i) Except as permitted in this paragraph (b)(2), a creditor shall not take into account an applicant's age (provided that the applicant has the capacity to enter into a binding contract) or whether an applicant's income derives from any public assistance program.

(ii) In an empirically derived, demonstrably and statistically sound credit scoring system, a creditor may use an applicant's age as a predictive variable, provided that the age of an elderly applicant is not assigned a negative factor or value.

(iii) In a judgmental system of evaluating creditworthiness, a creditor may consider an applicant's age or whether an applicant's income derives from any public assistance program only for the purposes of determining a pertinent element of creditworthiness.

(iv) In any system of evaluating creditworthiness, a creditor may consider the age of an elderly applicant when such age is used to favor the elderly applicant in extending credit.

(3) Childbearing, child-rearing. In evaluating creditworthiness, a creditor shall not use assumptions or aggregate statistics relating to the likelihood that any group of persons will bear or rear children or will, for that reason, receive diminished or interrupted income in the future.

(4) Telephone listing. A creditor shall not take into account whether there is a telephone listing in the name of applicant for consumer credit, but may take into account whether there is a telephone in the applicant's residence.

(5) Income. A creditor shall not discount or exclude from consideration the income of an applicant or the spouse of an applicant because of a prohibited basis or because the income is derived from part-time employment or is an annuity, pension, or other retirement benefit; a creditor may consider the amount and probable continuance of any income in evaluating an applicant's creditworthiness. When an applicant relies on alimony, child support, or separate maintenance payments in applying for credit, the creditor shall consider such payments as income to the extent that they are likely to be consistently made.

(6) Credit history. To the extent that a creditor considers credit history in evaluating the creditworthiness of similarly qualified applicants for a similar type and amount of credit, in evaluating an applicant's creditworthiness a creditor shall consider:

(i) The credit history, when available, of accounts designated as accounts that the applicant and the applicant's spouse are permitted to use or for which they are contractually liable:

(ii) On the applicant's request, any information the applicant may present that tends to indicate that the credit history being considered by the creditor does not accurately reflect the applicant's creditworthiness; and

(iii) On the applicant's request, the credit history, when available, of any account reported in the name of the applicant's spouse or former spouse that the applicant can demonstrate accurately reflects the applicant's creditworthiness.

(7) Immigration status. A creditor may consider whether an applicant is a permanent resident of the United States, the applicant's immigration status, and any additional information that may be necessary to ascertain the creditor's rights and remedies regarding repayment.

(c) State property laws. A creditor's consideration or application of state laws directly or indirectly affecting creditworthiness does not constitute unlawful discrimination for the purposes of the act or this regulation.

202.7 Rules concerning extensions of credits

(a) Individual accounts. A creditor shall not refuse to grant an individual account to a creditworthy applicant on the basis of sex, marital status, or any other prohibited basis.

(b) Designation of name. A creditor shall not refuse to allow an applicant to open or maintain an account in a birth-given first name and a surname that is the applicant's birth-given surname, the spouse's surname, or combined surname.

(c) Action concerning existing open-end accounts.

(1) Limitations. In the absence of the applicant's inability or unwillingness to repay, a creditor shall not take any of the following actions regarding an applicant who is contractually liable on an existing open-end account on the basis of the

applicant's reaching a certain age or retiring or on the basis of a change in the applicant's name or marital status:

(i) Require a reapplication, except as provided in paragraph (c)(2) of this section;

(ii) Change the terms of the account; or

(iii) Terminate the account.

(2) Requiring reapplication. A creditor may require a reapplication for an open-end account on the basis of a change in the marital status of an applicant who is contractually liable if the credit granted was based in whole or in part on income of the applicant's spouse and if information available to the creditor indicates that the applicant's income may not support the amount of credit currently available.

(d) Signature of spouse or other person.

(1) Rule for qualified applicant. Except as provided in this paragraph, a creditor shall not require the signature of an applicant's spouse or other person other than a joint applicant, on any credit instrument if the applicant qualified under the creditor's standards of creditworthiness for the amount and terms of the credit requested.

(2) Unsecured credit. If an applicant requests credit and relies in part upon property that the applicant owns jointly with another person to satisfy the creditor's standards of creditworthiness, the creditor may require the signature of the other person only on the instruments necessary, or reasonably believed by the creditor to be necessary, under the law of the state in which the property is located, to enable the creditor to reach the property being relied upon in the event of the death or default of the applicant.

(3) Unsecured credit—community property states. If a married applicant requests unsecured credit and resides in a community property state, or if the property upon which the applicant is relying is located in such a state, a creditor may require the signature of the spouse on any instrument necessary, or reasonably believed by the creditor to be necessary, under applicable state law to make the community property available to satisfy the debt in the event of default if:

(i) Applicable state law denies the applicant power to manage or control sufficient community property to qualify for the amount of credit requested under the creditor's standards of creditworthiness; and

(ii) The applicant does not have sufficient separate property to qualify for the amount of credit requested without regard to community property.

(4) Secured credit. If an applicant requests secured credit, a creditor may require the signature of the applicant's spouse or other person on any instrument necessary, or reasonably believed by the creditor to be necessary, under applicable state law to make the property being offered as security available to satisfy the debt in the event of default, for example, an instrument to create a valid lien, pass clear title, waive inchoate rights or assign earnings.

(5) Additional parties. If, under a creditor's standards of creditworthiness, the personal liability of an additional party is necessary to support the extension of the credit requested, a creditor may request a cosigner, a guarantor, or the like. The applicant's spouse may serve as an additional party, but the creditor shall not require that the spouse be the additional party.

(6) Rights of additional parties. A creditor shall not impose requirements upon an additional party that the creditor is prohibited from imposing upon an applicant under this section.

(e) Insurance. A creditor shall not refuse to extend credit and shall not terminate an account because life, health, accident, disability, or other credit-related insurance is not available on the basis of the applicant's age.

202.8 Special purpose credit programs

(a) Standards for programs. Subject to the provisions of paragraph (b) of this section, the act and this regulation permit a creditor to extend special purpose credit to applicants who meet eligibility requirements under the following types of credit programs:

(1) Any credit assistance program expressly authorized by federal or state law for the benefit of an economically disadvantaged class or persons;

(2) Any credit assistance program offered by a not-for-profit organization as defined under section 801(c) of the Internal Revenue Code of 1954, as amended, for the benefit of its members or for the benefit of an economically disadvantaged class of persons participates to meet special social needs, if—

(i) The program is established and administered pursuant to a written plan that identifies the class of persons that the program is designed to benefit and sets forth the procedures and standards for extending credit pursuant to the program; and

(ii) The program is established and administered to extend credit to a class of persons, who, under the organization's customary standards of creditworthiness, probably would not receive such credit or would receive it on less favorable terms than are ordinarily available to other applicants applying to the organization for a similar type and amount of credit.

(b) Rules in other sections.

(1) General applicability. All of the provisions of this regulation apply to each of the special purpose credit programs described in paragraph (a) of this section unless modified by this section.

(2) Common characteristics. A program described in paragraph (a)(2) or (a)(3) of this section qualifies as a special purpose credit program only if it was established and is administered so as not to discriminate against an applicant on any prohibited basis; however, all program participants may be required to share one or more common characteristics (for example, race, national origin, or sex) so long as the program was not established and is not administered with the purpose of evading the requirements of the act or this regulation.

(c) Special rule concerning requests and use of information. If participants in a special purpose credit program described in paragraph (a) of this section are required to possess one or more common characteristics (for example, race, national origin, or sex) and if the program otherwise satisfies the requirements of paragraph (a) of this section, a creditor may request and consider information regarding the common characteristics in determining the applicants eligibility for the program.
(d) Special rule in the case of financial need. If financial need is one of the criteria under a special purpose program described in paragraph (a) of this section, the creditor may request and consider, in determining an applicant's eligibility for the program, information regarding the applicant's marital status, alimony, child support, and separate maintenance income; and the spouse's financial resources. In addition, a creditor may obtain the signature of an applicant's spouse or other person on an application or credit instrument relating to a special purpose program if the signature is required by federal or state law.

2029 Notifications

(a) Notification of action taken, ECOA notice, and statement of specific reasons.

(1)When notification is required. A creditor shall notify an applicant of action taken within:

(i) 30 days after receiving a completed application concerning the creditor's approval of, counteroffer to, or adverse action on the application;
(ii) 30 days after taking adverse action on an incomplete application, unless notice is provided in accordance with paragraph (c) of this section;
(iii) 30 days after taking adverse action on an existing account; or
(iv) 90 days after notifying the applicant or a counteroffer if the applicant does not expressly accept or use the credit offered.

(2) Content of notification when adverse action is taken. A notification given to an applicant when adverse action is taken shall be in writing and shall contain: A statement of the action

taken; the name and address of the creditor; a statement of the provisions of section 701(a) of the act; the name and address of the federal agency that administers compliance with respect to the creditor; and either:

(i) A statement of specific reasons for the action taken; or

(ii) A disclosure of the applicant's right to a statement of specific reasons within 30 days, if the statement is requested within 60 days of the creditor's notification. The disclosure shall include the name, address, and telephone number of the person or office from which the statement of reasons can be obtained. If the creditor chooses to provide the reasons orally, the creditor shall also disclose the applicant's right to have them confirmed in writing within 30 days of receiving a written request for confirmation from the applicant.

(b) Form of ECOA notice and statement of specific reasons.

(1) ECOA notice. To satisfy the disclosure requirements of paragraph (a)(2) of this section regarding section 701(a) of the act, the creditor shall provide a notice that is substantially similar to the following: The Federal Equal Credit Opportunity Act prohibits creditors from discriminating against credit applicants on the basis of race, color, religion, national origin, sex, marital status, age (provided the applicant has the capacity to enter into a binding contract); because all or part of the applicant's income derives from public assistance programs; or because the applicant has in good faith exercised any right under the Consumer Credit Protection Act. The federal agency that administers compliance with this law concerning this creditor is (name and address as specified by the appropriate agency listed in Appendix A of this regulation).

(2) Statement of specific reasons. The statement of reasons for adverse action required by paragraph (a)(2)(i) of this section must be specific and indicate the principal reason(s) for the adverse action. Statements that the adverse action

was based on the creditor's internal standards policies or that the applicant failed to achieve the qualifying score on the creditor's credit scoring system are insufficient.

(c) Incomplete applications.

(1) Notice alternatives. Within 30 days after receiving an application that is incomplete regarding matters that an applicant can complete, the creditor shall notify the applicant either:

(i) Of action taken, in accordance with paragraph (a) of this section; or

(ii) Of the incompleteness, in accordance with paragraph (e)(2) of this section.

(2) Notice of incompleteness. If additional information is needed from an applicant, the creditor shall send a written notice to the applicant specifying the information needed, designating a reasonable period of time for the applicant to provide the information, and informing the applicant that failure to provide the information will result in no further consideration being given to the application. The creditor shall have no further obligation under this section if the applicant fails to respond within the designated time period. If the applicant supplies the requested information within the designated time period, the creditor shall take action on the application and notify the applicant in accordance with paragraph (a) of this section.

(3) Oral requests for information. At its option, a creditor may inform the applicant orally of the need for additional information; but if the application remains incomplete the creditor shall send a notice in accordance with paragraph (c)(1) of this section.

(4) Oral notifications by small-volume creditors. The requirements of this section (including statements of specific reasons) are satisfied by oral notifications in the case of any creditor that did not receive more than 150 applications during the preceding calendar year.

(e) Withdrawal of approved applications. When an applicant submits an application and the parties contemplate that the applicant will inquire about its status, if the creditor approves the application and the applicant has not

inquired within 30 days after applying, the creditor may treat the application as withdrawn and need not comply with paragraph (a)(1) of this section.
(f) Multiple applicants. When an application involves more than one applicant, notification need only by given to one of them, but must be given to the primary applicant where one is readily apparent.
(g) Applications submitted through a third party. When an application is made on behalf of an applicant to more than one creditor and the applicant expressly accepts or uses credit offered by one of the creditors, notification of action taken by any of the other creditors is not required. If no credit is offered or if the applicant does not expressly accept or use any credit offered, each creditor taking adverse action must comply with this section, directly or through a third party. A notice given by a third party shall disclose the identity of each creditor on whose behalf the notice is given.

202.10 Furnishing of credit information

(a) Designation of accounts. A creditor that furnished credit information shall designate:

(1) Any new account to reflect the participation of both spouses if the applicant's spouse is permitted to use or is contractually liable on the account (other than as a guarantor, surety, endorser, or similar party);
(2) Any existing account to reflect such participation, within 90 days after receiving a written request to do so from one of the spouses.

(b) Routine reports to consumer reporting agency. If a creditor furnishes credit information to a consumer reporting agency concerning an account designated to reflect the participation of both spouses, the creditor shall furnish the information in a manner that will enable the agency to provide access to the information in the name of each spouse.
(c) Reporting in response to inquiry. If a creditor furnishes credit information in response to an inquiry concerning an account designated to reflect the participation of both spouses, the creditor shall furnish the information in the name of the spouse about whom the information is requested.

202.11 Relations to state law

(a) Inconsistent state laws. Except as otherwise provided in this section, this regulation alters, affects, or preempts only those state laws that are inconsistent with the act and this regulation and then only to the extent of the inconsistency. A state law is not inconsistent if it is more protective of an applicant.

(b) Preempted provisions of state law.

(1) A state law is deemed to be inconsistent with the requirements of the act and this regulation and less protective of an applicant within the meaning of section 706(f) of the act to the extent that the law:

(i) Requires or permits a practice or act prohibited by the act or this regulation;

(ii) Prohibits the individual extension of consumer credit to both parties to a marriage if each spouse individually and voluntarily applies for such credit;

(iii) Prohibits inquiries or collection of data required to comply with the act or this regulation;

(iv) Prohibits asking or considering age in an empirically derived, demonstrably and statistically sound credit scoring system to determine a pertinent element of creditworthiness, or to favor an elderly applicant; or

(v) Prohibits inquiries necessary to establish or administer as special purpose credit program as defined by 202.8.

(2) A creditor, state, or other interested party may request the Board to determine whether a state law is inconsistent with the requirements of the act and this regulation.

(c) Laws on finance charges, loan ceilings. If married applicants voluntarily apply for and obtain individual accounts with the same creditor, the accounts shall not be aggregated or otherwise combined for purposes of determining permissible finance charges or loan ceilings under any federal or state law. Permissible loan ceiling laws shall be construed to permit each spouse to become individually liable up to the amount of the loan ceilings, less the amount for which the applicant is jointly liable.

(d) State and federal laws not affected. This section does not alter or annul any provision of state property laws, laws relating to the disposition of decedents' estates, or federal or state banking regulation directed only toward insuring the solvency of financial institutions.

(e) Exemption for state-regulated transactions.

(1) Applications. A state may apply to the Board for an exemption from the requirements of the act and this regulation for any class of credit transactions within the state. The Board will grant such an exemption if the Board determines that:

(i) The class of credit transactions is subject to state law requirements substantially similar to the act and this regulation or that applicants are afforded greater protection under state law; and

(ii) There is adequate provision for state enforcement.

(2) Liability and enforcement.

(i) No exemption will extend to the civil liability provisions of section 706 or the administrative enforcement provisions of section 704 of the act.

(ii) After an exemption has been granted, the requirements of the applicable state law (except for additional requirements not imposed by federal law) will constitute the requirements of the act and this regulation.

202.12 Record retention

(a) Retention of prohibited information. A creditor may retain in its files information that is prohibited by the act or this regulation in evaluating applications, without violating the act or this regulation, if the information is obtained:

(1) From any source prior to March 25, 1977;

(2) From consumer reporting agencies, an applicant, or others without the specific request of the creditor; or

(3) As required to monitor compliance with the act and this regulation or other federal or state statutes or regulations.

(b) Preservation of records.

(1) Applications. For 25 months after the date that a creditor notifies an applicant of action taken on an application or incompleteness, the creditor shall retain in original form or a copy thereof—

(i) any application that it receives, any information required to be obtained concerning characteristics of the applicant to monitor compliance with the act and this regulation or other similar law, and any other written or recorded information used in evaluating the application and not returned to the applicant at the applicant's request;

(ii) A copy of the following documents if furnished to the applicant in written form (or, if furnished orally, any notation or memorandum made by the creditor):

(A) The notification of action taken; and

(B) The statement of specific reasons for adverse action; and

(iii) Any written statement submitted by the applicants alleging a violation of the act or this regulation.

(2) Existing accounts. For 25 months after the date that a creditor notifies an applicant of adverse action regarding an existing account, the creditor shall retain as to that account, in original form or a copy thereof—

(i) Any written or recorded information concerning the adverse action: and

(ii) Any written statement submitted by the applicant alleging a violation of the act or this regulation.

(3) Other applications. For 25 months after the date that a creditor receives an application for which the creditor is not required to comply with the notification requirements of 202.9, the creditor shall retain all written or recorded information in its possession concerning the applicant, including any notation of action taken.

(4) Enforcement of proceedings and investigations. A creditor shall retain the information specified in this section beyond 25 months if it has actual notice that it is under investigation or is subject to an enforcement proceeding for an alleged violation of the act of this violation of the act or this regulation by the Attorney General of the United States or by an enforcement agency charged with monitoring that creditor's compliance with the act and this regulation, or if it has been served with notice of an action filed pursuant to section 706 of the act and 202.14 of this regulation. The creditor shall retain the information until final disposition of the matter, unless an earlier time is allowed by order of the agency or court.

202.13 Information for monitoring purposes

(a) Information to be requested. A creditor that receives an application for credit primarily for the purchase or refinancing of a dwelling occupied by the applicant as a principal residence, where the extension of credit will be secured by the dwelling, shall request as part of the application the following information regarding the applicant(s):

(1) Race or national origin, using the categories American Indian or Alaskan Native; Asian or Pacific Islander; Black; White; Hispanic; Other (specify);

(2) Sex;

(3) Marital status, using the categories married, unmarried, and separated; and

(4) Age.

"Dwelling" means a residential structure that contains one to four units, whether or not that structure is attached to real property. The term includes, but is not limited to, an individual condominium or cooperative unit, and a mobile or other manufactured home.

(b) Obtaining of information. Questions regarding race or national origin, sex, marital status, and age may be listed, at the creditor's option, on the application form or on a separate form that refers to the application. The applicant(s) shall be asked but not required to supply the requested information. If the applicant(s) chooses not to provide the information or any part of it, that fact shall be noted on the form. The creditor shall then also note on the form, to the extent possible, the race or national origin and sex of the applicant(s) on the basis of visual observation or surname.

(c) Disclosure to applicant(s). The creditor shall inform the applicant(s) that the information regarding race or national origin, sex, marital status, and age is being requested by the federal government for the purpose of monitoring compliance with federal statutes that prohibit creditors from discriminating against applicants on those bases. The creditor shall also inform the applicant(s) that if the applicant(s) chooses not to provide the information, the creditor is required to note the race or national origin and sex on the basis of visual observation or surname.

(d) Substitutive-monitoring program. A monitoring program required by an agency charged with administrative enforcement under section 704 of the act may be substituted for the requirements contained in paragraphs (a), (b), and (c).

202.14 Enforcement, penalties, and liabilities

(a) Administrative enforcement.

(1) As set forth more fully in section 704 of the act, administrative enforcement of the act and this regulation regarding certain creditors is assigned to the Comptroller of the Currency, Board of Governors of the Federal Reserve System, Board of Directors of the Federal Deposit Insurance Corporation, Federal Home Loan Bank Board (acting directly or through the Federal Savings and Loan Insurance Corporation), National Credit Union Administration, Interstate Commerce Commission, Secretary of Agriculture, Farm Credit Administration, Securities and Exchange Commission, Small Business Administration, and Secretary of Transportation.

(2) Except to the extent that administrative enforcement is specifically assigned to other authorities, compliance with the requirements imposed under the act and this regulation is enforced by the Federal Trade Commission.

(b) Penalties and Liabilities.

(1) Sections 706(a) and (b) and 702(g) of the act provide that any creditor that fails to comply with a requirement imposed by the act or this regulation is subject to civil liability for actual and punitive damages in individual or class actions.

Pursuant to sections 704(b), (c), and (d) and 702(g) of the act, violations of the act or regulations also constitute violations of other federal laws. Liability for punitive damages is restricted to nongovernmental entities and is limited to $10,000 in individual actions and the lesser of $50,000 or 1 percent of the creditor's net worth in class actions, section 706(c) provides for equitable and declaratory relief and section 706(d) authorizes the awarding of costs and reasonable attorney's fees to an aggrieved applicant in a successful action.

(2) As provided in section 706(f), a civil action under the act or this regulation may be brought in the appropriate United States district court without regard to the amount in controversy or in any other court of competent jurisdiction within two years after the date of the occurrence of the violation, or within one year after the commencement of an administrative enforcement proceeding or of a civil action brought by the Attorney General of the United States within two years after the alleged violation.

(3) Sections 706(g) and (h) provide that, if an agency responsible for administrative enforcement is unable to obtain compliance with the act or this regulation, it may refer the matter to the Attorney General of the United States. On referral, or whenever the Attorney General has reason to believe that one or more creditors are engaged in a pattern or practice in violation of the act or this regulation, the Attorney General may bring a civil action.

(c) Failure of compliance. A creditor's failure to comply with 202.6(b)(6), 202.9, 202.10, 202.12 or 202.13 is not a violation if it results from an inadvertent error. On discovering an error under 202.9 and 202.10, the creditor shall correct it as soon as possible. If a creditor inadvertently obtains the monitoring information regarding the race or national origin and sex of the applicant in a dwelling-related transaction not covered by 202.13, the creditor may act on and retain the application without violating the regulation.

Appendix A: Federal Enforcement Agencies

The following list indicates the federal agencies that enforce Regulation B for particular classes of creditors. Any questions concerning a particular creditor should be directed to its enforcement agency.

National banks

Comptroller of the Currency
Consumer Examinations Division
Washington, DC 20219

State member banks

Federal Reserve Bank serving the district in which the state member bank is located.

Nonmember insured banks

Federal Deposit Insurance Corporation
Regional Director for the region in which the nonmember insured bank is located.
Savings institutions insured by the FSLIC and members for the FHLB system (except for savings banks insured by FDIC)
The Federal Home Loan Bank Board Supervisory Agent in the district in which the institution is located.

Federal credit unions

Regional Office of the National Credit Union Administration serving the area in which the federal credit union is located.

Creditors subject to Interstate Commerce Commission

Office Proceedings
Interstate Commerce Commission
Washington, DC 20523

Creditors subject to Packers and Stockyards Act

Nearest Packers and Stockyards Administration area supervisor
U.S. Small Business Administration
1441 L Street, N.W.
Washington, DC 20416

Appendix C

The Fair Debt Collection Practices Act (As amended by Public Law 104-208, 110 Stat. 3009, Sept. 30, 1996)

To amend the Consumer Credit Protection Act to prohibit abusive practices by debt collectors.

Be it enacted by the Senate and House of Representatives of the United States of America in Congress assembled, that the Consumer Credit Protection Act (15 U.S.C. 1601 et seq.) is amended by adding at the end thereof the following new title:

Title VIII - Debt Collection Practices [Fair Debt Collection Practices Act]

Sections

§ 801. Short Title [15 USC 1601 note]

This title may be cited as the "Fair Debt Collection Practices Act."

§ 802. Congressional findings and declaration of purpose [15 USC 1692]

(a) There is abundant evidence of the use of abusive, deceptive, and unfair debt collection practices by many debt collectors. Abusive debt collection practices contribute to the number of personal bankruptcies, to marital instability, to the loss of jobs, and to invasions of individual privacy.
(b) Existing laws and procedures for redressing these injuries are inadequate to protect consumers.
(c) Means other than misrepresentation or other abusive debt collection practices are available for the effective collection of debts.
(d) Abusive debt collection practices are carried on to a substantial extent in interstate commerce and through means and instrumentalities of such commerce. Even where abusive debt collection practices are purely intrastate

in character, they nevertheless directly affect interstate commerce.
(e) It is the purpose of this title to eliminate abusive debt collection practices by debt collectors, to insure that those debt collectors who refrain from using abusive debt collection practices are not competitively disadvantaged, and to promote consistent State action to protect consumers against debt collection abuses.

§ 803. Definitions [15 USC 1692a]

As used in this title —

(1) The term "Commission" means the Federal Trade Commission.
(2) The term "communication" means the conveying of information regarding a debt directly or indirectly to any person through any medium.
(3) The term "consumer" means any natural person obligated or allegedly obligated to pay any debt.
(4) The term "creditor" means any person who offers or extends credit creating a debt or to whom a debt is owed, but such term does not include any person to the extent that he receives an assignment or transfer of a debt in default solely for the purpose of facilitating collection of such debt for another.
(5) The term "debt" means any obligation or alleged obligation of a consumer to pay money arising out of a transaction in which the money, property, insurance or services which are the subject of the transaction are primarily for personal, family, or household purposes, whether or not such obligation has been reduced to judgment.
(6) The term "debt collector" means any person who uses any instrumentality of interstate commerce or the mails in any business the principal purpose of which is the collection of any debts, or who regularly collects or attempts to collect, directly or indirectly, debts owed or due or asserted to be owed or due another. Notwithstanding the exclusion provided by clause (F) of the last sentence of this paragraph, the term includes any creditor who, in the process of collecting his own debts, uses any name other than his own which would

indicate that a third person is collecting or attempting to collect such debts. For the purpose of section 808(6), such term also includes any person who uses any instrumentality of interstate commerce or the mails in any business the principal purpose of which is the enforcement of security interests. The term does not include —

(A) any officer or employee of a creditor while, in the name of the creditor, collecting debts for such creditor;

(B) any person while acting as a debt collector for another person, both of whom are related by common ownership or affiliated by corporate control, if the person acting as a debt collector does so only for persons to whom it is so related or affiliated and if the principal business of such person is not the collection of debts;

(C) any officer or employee of the United States or any State to the extent that collecting or attempting to collect any debt is in the performance of his official duties;

(D) any person while serving or attempting to serve legal process on any other person in connection with the judicial enforcement of any debt;

(E) any nonprofit organization which, at the request of consumers, performs bona fide consumer credit counseling and assists consumers in the liquidation of their debts by receiving payments from such consumers and distributing such amounts to creditors; and

(F) any person collecting or attempting to collect any debt owed or due or asserted to be owed or due another to the extent such activity (i) is incidental to a bona fide fiduciary obligation or a bona fide escrow arrangement; (ii) concerns a debt which was originated by such person; (iii) concerns a debt which was not in default at the time it was obtained by such person; or (iv) concerns a debt obtained by such person as a secured party in a commercial credit transaction involving the creditor.

(7) The term "location information" means a consumer's place of abode and his telephone number at such place, or his place of employment.

(8) The term "State" means any State, territory, or possession of the United States, the District of Columbia, the Commonwealth of Puerto Rico, or any political subdivision of any of the foregoing.

§ 804. Acquisition of location information [15 USC 1692b]

Any debt collector communicating with any person other than the consumer for the purpose of acquiring location information about the consumer shall —

(1) identify himself, state that he is confirming or correcting location information concerning the consumer, and, only if expressly requested, identify his employer;

(2) not state that such consumer owes any debt;

(3) not communicate with any such person more than once unless requested to do so by such person or unless the debt collector reasonably believes that the earlier response of such person is erroneous or incomplete and that such person now has correct or complete location information;

(4) not communicate by post card;

(5) not use any language or symbol on any envelope or in the contents of any communication effected by the mails or telegram that indicates that the debt collector is in the debt collection business or that the communication relates to the collection of a debt; and

(6) after the debt collector knows the consumer is represented by an attorney with regard to the subject debt and has knowledge of, or can readily ascertain, such attorney's name and address, not communicate with any person other than

that attorney, unless the attorney fails to respond within a reasonable period of time to the communication from the debt collector.

§ 805. Communication in connection with debt collection [15 USC 1692c]

(a) Communication with the consumer generally. Without the prior consent of the consumer given directly to the debt collector or the express permission of a court of competent jurisdiction, a debt collector may not communicate with a consumer in connection with the collection of any debt —

(1) at any unusual time or place or a time or place known or which should be known to be inconvenient to the consumer. In the absence of knowledge of circumstances to the contrary, a debt collector shall assume that the convenient time for communicating with a consumer is after 8 o'clock antemeridian and before 9 o'clock postmeridian, local time at the consumer's location;

(2) if the debt collector knows the consumer is represented by an attorney with respect to such debt and has knowledge of, or can readily ascertain, such attorney's name and address, unless the attorney fails to respond within a reasonable period of time to a communication from the debt collector or unless the attorney consents to direct communication with the consumer; or

(3) at the consumer's place of employment if the debt collector knows or has reason to know that the consumer's employer prohibits the consumer from receiving such communication.

(b) Communication with third parties. Except as provided in section 804, without the prior consent of the consumer given directly to the debt collector, or the express permission of a court of competent jurisdiction, or as reasonably necessary to effectuate a postjudgment judicial remedy, a debt collector may not communicate, in connection with the collection of any debt, with any person other than a consumer, his attorney, a consumer reporting agency if otherwise permitted by law, the creditor, the attorney of the creditor, or the attorney of the debt collector.

(c) Ceasing communication. If a consumer notifies a debt collector in writing that the consumer refuses to pay a debt or that the consumer wishes the debt collector to cease further communication with the consumer, the debt collector shall not communicate further with the consumer with respect to such debt, except —

(1) to advise the consumer that the debt collector's further efforts are being terminated;

(2) to notify the consumer that the debt collector or creditor may invoke specified remedies which are ordinarily invoked by such debt collector or creditor; or

(3) where applicable, to notify the consumer that the debt collector or creditor intends to invoke a specified remedy.

If such notice from the consumer is made by mail, notification shall be complete upon receipt.

(d) For the purpose of this section, the term "consumer" includes the consumer's spouse, parent (if the consumer is a minor), guardian, executor, or administrator.

§ 806. Harassment or abuse [15 USC 1692d]

A debt collector may not engage in any conduct the natural consequence of which is to harass, oppress, or abuse any person in connection with the collection of a debt. Without limiting the general application of the foregoing, the following conduct is a violation of this section:

(1) The use or threat of use of violence or other criminal means to harm the physical person, reputation, or property of any person.

(2) The use of obscene or profane language or language the natural consequence of which is to abuse the hearer or reader.

(3) The publication of a list of consumers who allegedly refuse to pay debts, except to a consumer reporting agency or to persons meeting the requirements of section 603(f) or 604(3)[1] of this Act.

(4) The advertisement for sale of any debt to coerce payment of the debt.

(5) Causing a telephone to ring or engaging any person in telephone conversation repeatedly or continuously with intent to annoy, abuse, or harass any person at the called number.

(6) Except as provided in section 804, the placement of telephone calls without meaningful disclosure of the caller's identity.

§ 807. False or misleading representations [15 USC 1962e]

A debt collector may not use any false, deceptive, or misleading representation or means in connection with the collection of any debt. Without limiting the general application of the foregoing, the following conduct is a violation of this section:

(1) The false representation or implication that the debt collector is vouched for, bonded by, or affiliated with the United States or any State, including the use of any badge, uniform, or facsimile thereof.

(2) The false representation of —

(A) the character, amount, or legal status of any debt; or

(B) any services rendered or compensation which may be lawfully received by any debt collector for the collection of a debt.

(3) The false representation or implication that any individual is an attorney or that any communication is from an attorney.

(4) The representation or implication that nonpayment of any debt will result in the arrest or imprisonment of any person or the seizure, garnishment, attachment, or sale of any property or wages of any person unless such action is lawful and the debt collector or creditor intends to take such action.

(5) The threat to take any action that cannot legally be taken or that is not intended to be taken.

(6) The false representation or implication that a sale, referral, or other transfer of any interest in a debt shall cause the consumer to —

(A) lose any claim or defense to payment of the debt; or

(B) become subject to any practice prohibited by this title.

(7) The false representation or implication that the consumer committed any crime or other conduct in order to disgrace the consumer.

(8) Communicating or threatening to communicate to any person credit information which is known or which should be known to be false, including the failure to communicate that a disputed debt is disputed.

(9) The use or distribution of any written communication which simulates or is falsely represented to be a document authorized, issued, or approved by any court, official, or agency of the United States or any State, or which creates a false impression as to its source, authorization, or approval.

(10) The use of any false representation or deceptive means to collect or attempt to collect any debt or to obtain information concerning a consumer.

(11) The failure to disclose in the initial written communication with the consumer and, in addition, if the initial communication with the consumer is oral, in that initial oral communication, that the debt collector is attempting to collect a debt and that any information obtained will be used for that purpose, and the failure to disclose in subsequent communications that the communication is from a debt collector, except that this paragraph shall not apply to a formal pleading made in connection with a legal action.

(12) The false representation or implication that accounts have been turned over to innocent purchasers for value.

(13) The false representation or implication that documents are legal process.

(14) The use of any business, company, or organization name other than the true name of the debt collector's business, company, or organization.

(15) The false representation or implication that documents are not legal process forms or do not require action by the consumer.

(16) The false representation or implication that a debt collector operates or is employed by a consumer reporting agency as defined by section 603(f) of this Act.

§ 808. Unfair practices [15 USC 1692f]

A debt collector may not use unfair or unconscionable means to collect or attempt to collect any debt. Without limiting the general application of the foregoing, the following conduct is a violation of this section:

(1) The collection of any amount (including any interest, fee, charge, or expense incidental to the principal obligation) unless such amount is expressly authorized by the agreement creating the debt or permitted by law.

(2) The acceptance by a debt collector from any person of a check or other payment instrument postdated by more than five days unless such person is notified in writing of the debt collector's intent to deposit such check or instrument not more than ten nor less than three business days prior to such deposit.

(3) The solicitation by a debt collector of any postdated check or other postdated payment instrument for the purpose of threatening or instituting criminal prosecution.

(4) Depositing or threatening to deposit any postdated check or other postdated payment instrument prior to the date on such check or instrument.

(5) Causing charges to be made to any person for communications by concealment of the true propose of the communication. Such charges include, but are not limited to, collect telephone calls and telegram fees.

(6) Taking or threatening to take any nonjudicial action to effect dispossession or disablement of property if—

(A) there is no present right to possession of the property claimed as collateral through an enforceable security interest;

(B) there is no present intention to take possession of the property; or

(C) the property is exempt by law from such dispossession or disablement.

(7) Communicating with a consumer regarding a debt by post card.

(8) Using any language or symbol, other than the debt collector's address, on any envelope when communicating with a consumer by use of the mails or by telegram, except that a debt collector may use his business name if such name does not indicate that he is in the debt collection business.

§ 809. Validation of debts [15 USC 1692g]

(a) Within five days after the initial communication with a consumer in connection with the collection of any debt, a debt collector shall, unless the following information is contained in the initial communication or the consumer has paid the debt, send the consumer a written notice containing —

(1) the amount of the debt;

(2) the name of the creditor to whom the debt is owed;

(3) a statement that unless the consumer, within thirty days after receipt of the notice, disputes the validity of the debt, or any portion thereof, the debt will be assumed to be valid by the debt collector;

(4) a statement that if the consumer notifies the debt collector in writing within the thirty-day period that the debt, or any portion thereof, is disputed, the debt collector will obtain verification of the debt or a copy of a judgment against the consumer and a copy of such verification or judgment will be mailed to the consumer by the debt collector; and

(5) a statement that, upon the consumer's written request within the thirty-day period, the debt collector will provide the consumer with the name and address of the original creditor, if different from the current creditor.

(b) If the consumer notifies the debt collector in writing within the thirty-day period described in subsection (a) that the debt, or any portion thereof, is disputed, or that the consumer requests the name and address of the original creditor, the debt collector shall cease collection of the debt, or any disputed portion thereof, until the debt collector obtains verification of the debt or any copy of a judgment, or the name and address of the original creditor, and a copy of such verification or judgment, or name and address of the original creditor, is mailed to the consumer by the debt collector.

(c) The failure of a consumer to dispute the validity of a debt under this section may not be construed by any court as an admission of liability by the consumer.

§ 810. Multiple debts [15 USC 1692h]

If any consumer owes multiple debts and makes any single payment to any debt collector with respect to such debts, such debt collector may not apply such payment to any debt which is disputed by the consumer and, where applicable, shall apply such payment in accordance with the consumer's directions.

§ 811. Legal actions by debt collectors [15 USC 1692i]

(a) Any debt collector who brings any legal action on a debt against any consumer shall —

(1) in the case of an action to enforce an interest in real property securing the consumer's obligation, bring such action only in a judicial district or similar legal entity in which such real property is located; or

(2) in the case of an action not described in paragraph (1), bring such action only in the judicial district or similar legal entity —

(A) in which such consumer signed the contract sued upon; or

(B) in which such consumer resides at the commencement of the action.

(b) Nothing in this title shall be construed to authorize the bringing of legal actions by debt collectors.

§ 812. Furnishing certain deceptive forms [15 USC 1692j]

(a) It is unlawful to design, compile, and furnish any form knowing that such form would be used to create the false belief in a consumer that a person other than the creditor of such consumer is participating in the collection of or in an attempt to collect a debt such consumer allegedly owes such creditor, when in fact such person is not so participating.

(b) Any person who violates this section shall be liable to the same extent and in the same manner as a debt collector is liable under section 813 for failure to comply with a provision of this title.

§ 813. Civil liability [15 USC 1692k]

(a) Except as otherwise provided by this section, any debt collector who fails to comply with any provision of this title with respect to any person is liable to such person in an amount equal to the sum of —

(1) any actual damage sustained by such person as a result of such failure;

(2) (A) in the case of any action by an individual, such additional damages as the court may allow, but not exceeding $1,000; or

(B) in the case of a class action, (i) such amount for each named plaintiff as could be recovered under subparagraph (A), and (ii) such amount as the court may allow for all other class members, without regard to a minimum individual recovery, not to exceed the lesser of $500,000 or 1 per centum of the net worth of the debt collector; and

(3) in the case of any successful action to enforce the foregoing liability, the costs of the action, together with a reasonable attorney's fee as determined by the court. On a finding by the court that an action under this section was brought in bad faith and for the purpose of harassment, the court may award to the defendant attorney's fees reasonable in relation to the work expended and costs.

(b) In determining the amount of liability in any action under subsection (a), the court shall consider, among other relevant factors —

(1) in any individual action under subsection (a)(2)(A), the frequency and persistence of noncompliance by the debt collector, the nature of such noncompliance, and the extent to which such noncompliance was intentional; or

(2) in any class action under subsection (a)(2)(B), the frequency and persistence of noncompliance by the debt collector, the nature of such noncompliance, the resources of the debt collector, the number of persons adversely affected, and the extent to which the debt collector's noncompliance was intentional.

(c) A debt collector may not be held liable in any action brought under this title if the debt collector shows by a preponderance of evidence that the violation was not intentional and resulted from a bona fide error notwithstanding the maintenance of procedures reasonably adapted to avoid any such error.

(d) An action to enforce any liability created by this title may be brought in any appropriate United States district court without regard to the amount in controversy, or in any other court of competent jurisdiction, within one year from the date on which the violation occurs.
(e) No provision of this section imposing any liability shall apply to any act done or omitted in good faith in conformity with any advisory opinion of the Commission, notwithstanding that after such act or omission has occurred, such opinion is amended, rescinded, or determined by judicial or other authority to be invalid for any reason.

§ 814. Administrative enforcement [15 USC 1692*l*]

(a) Compliance with this title shall be enforced by the Commission, except to the extend that enforcement of the requirements imposed under this title is specifically committed to another agency under subsection (b). For purpose of the exercise by the Commission of its functions and powers under the Federal Trade Commission Act, a violation of this title shall be deemed an unfair or deceptive act or practice in violation of that Act. All of the functions and powers of the Commission under the Federal Trade Commission Act are available to the Commission to enforce compliance by any person with this title, irrespective of whether that person is engaged in commerce or meets any other jurisdictional tests in the Federal Trade Commission Act, including the power to enforce the provisions of this title in the same manner as if the violation had been a violation of a Federal Trade Commission trade regulation rule.
(b) Compliance with any requirements imposed under this title shall be enforced under —

> (1) section 8 of the Federal Deposit Insurance Act, in the case of —
>
> > (A) national banks, by the Comptroller of the Currency;
> > (B) member banks of the Federal Reserve System (other than national banks), by the Federal Reserve Board; and
> > (C) banks the deposits or accounts of which are insured by the Federal Deposit Insurance Corporation (other than members of the Federal Reserve System), by the Board of

Directors of the Federal Deposit Insurance Corporation;

(2) section 5(d) of the Home Owners Loan Act of 1933, section 407 of the National Housing Act, and sections 6(i) and 17 of the Federal Home Loan Bank Act, by the Federal Home Loan Bank Board (acting directing or through the Federal Savings and Loan Insurance Corporation), in the case of any institution subject to any of those provisions;

(3) the Federal Credit Union Act, by the Administrator of the National Credit Union Administration with respect to any Federal credit union;

(4) subtitle IV of Title 49, by the Interstate Commerce Commission with respect to any common carrier subject to such subtitle;

(5) the Federal Aviation Act of 1958, by the Secretary of Transportation with respect to any air carrier or any foreign air carrier subject to that Act; and

(6) the Packers and Stockyards Act, 1921 (except as provided in section 406 of that Act), by the Secretary of Agriculture with respect to any activities subject to that Act.

(c) For the purpose of the exercise by any agency referred to in subsection (b) of its powers under any Act referred to in that subsection, a violation of any requirement imposed under this title shall be deemed to be a violation of a requirement imposed under that Act. In addition to its powers under any provision of law specifically referred to in subsection (b), each of the agencies referred to in that subsection may exercise, for the purpose of enforcing compliance with any requirement imposed under this title any other authority conferred on it by law, except as provided in subsection (d).

(d) Neither the Commission nor any other agency referred to in subsection (b) may promulgate trade regulation rules or other regulations with respect to the collection of debts by debt collectors as defined in this title.

§ 815. Reports to Congress by the Commission [15 USC 1692m]

(a) Not later than one year after the effective date of this title and at one-year intervals thereafter, the Commission shall make reports to the Congress concerning the administration of its functions under this title, including such recommendations as the Commission deems necessary or appropriate. In addition, each report of the Commission shall include its assessment of the extent to which compliance with this title is being achieved and a summary of the enforcement actions taken by the Commission under section 814 of this title.

(b) In the exercise of its functions under this title, the Commission may obtain upon request the views of any other Federal agency which exercises enforcement functions under section 814 of this title.

§ 816. Relation to State laws [15 USC 1692n]

This title does not annul, alter, or affect, or exempt any person subject to the provisions of this title from complying with the laws of any State with respect to debt collection practices, except to the extent that those laws are inconsistent with any provision of this title, and then only to the extent of the inconsistency. For purposes of this section, a State law is not inconsistent with this title if the protection such law affords any consumer is greater than the protection provided by this title.

§ 817. Exemption for State regulation [15 USC 1692o]

The Commission shall by regulation exempt from the requirements of this title any class of debt collection practices within any State if the Commission determines that under the law of that State that class of debt collection practices is subject to requirements substantially similar to those imposed by this title, and that there is adequate provision for enforcement.

§ 818. Effective date [15 USC 1692 note]

This title takes effect upon the expiration of six months after the date of its enactment, but section 809 shall apply only with respect to debts for which the initial attempt to collect occurs after such effective date.

Approved September 20, 1977

Endnotes

1. So in original; however, should read "604(a)(3)."

Legislative history

- ❑ Public Law 95-109 [H.R. 5294]
- ❑ House Report No. 95-131 (Comm. on Banking, Finance, and Urban Affairs).
- ❑ Senate Report No. 95-382 (Comm. on Banking, Housing, and Urban Affairs).
- ❑ Congressional Record, Vol. 123 (1977):
  Apr. 4, considered and passed House.
  Aug. 5, considered and passed Senate, amended.
  Sept. 8, House agreed to Senate amendment.
- ❑ Weekly Compilation of Presidential Documents, Vol. 13, No. 39:
- ❑ Sept. 20, Presidential statement.

Amendments

- ❑ Section 621, Subsections (b)(3), (b)(4) and (b)(5) were amended to transfer certain administrative enforcement responsibilities, pursuant to Pub. L. 95-473, § 3(b), Oct. 17, 1978. 92 Stat. 166; Pub. L. 95-630, Title V. § 501, November 10, 1978, 92 Stat. 3680; Pub. L. 98-443, § 9(h), Oct. 4, 1984, 98 Stat. 708.
- ❑ Section 803, Subsection (6), defining "debt collector," was amended to repeal the attorney at law exemption at former Section (6)(F) and to redesignate Section 803(6)(G) pursuant to Pub. L. 99-361, July 9, 1986, 100 Stat. 768. For legislative history, *see* H.R. 237, House Report No. 99-405 (Comm. on Banking, Finance and Urban Affairs). Congressional Record: Vol. 131 (1985): Dec. 2, considered and passed House. Vol. 132 (1986): June 26, considered and passed Senate.
- ❑ Section 807, Subsection (11), was amended to affect when debt collectors must state (a) that they are attempting to collect a debt and (b) that information obtained will be used for that purpose, pursuant to Pub. L. 104-208 § 2305, 110 Stat. 3009 (Sept. 30, 1996).

Appendix D

Where to get help

- ❑ **Debtors Anonymous.** An effective support group for anyone with a debt or spending problem based on the 12 steps of Alcoholics Anonymous. There are no dues or fees. For a meeting list or to form a chapter in your area, contact the General Service Office at P.O. Box 920888, Needham, MA 02492-0009. Call (781) 453-2743 or fax (781) 453-2745. The Web site address is `www.debtorsanonymous.org`.
- ❑ **Consumer Action.** An education and advocacy organization specializing in credit, finance, and telecommunications issues. Offers a multilingual consumer complaint hotline, free information on its surveys of banks and long-distance telephone companies, and consumer education materials in as many as eight languages. Write to 7171 Market St., Suite 310, San Francisco, CA 94103, or call the consumer complaint hotline at (415) 777-9365 (10 am to 2 pm PST) or the general hotline at (213) 624-8327. The fax number is (415) 777-5267 (TTY: (415) 777-9456).

- **National Consumer Law Center** (NCLC). An advocacy and research organization focusing on the needs of low-income consumers. Represents the interests of consumers in court, before administrative agencies, and before legislatures. Contact: 18 Tremont St., Boston, MA 02108 or call (617) 523-8010, fax (617) 523-7398. The Web site address is `www.consumerlaw.org`.
- **National Institute for Consumer Education** (NICE). A consumer education resource and professional development center for K-12 classroom teachers, business, government, labor and community educators. Conducts training programs, develops teaching guides and resource lists, and manages a national clearinghouse of consumer educational materials, including videos, software programs, textbooks, and curriculum guides. Contact NICE at Eastern Michigan University, 207 Rackham Building, Ypsilanti, MI 48197 or call (313) 487-2292, fax (313) 487-7153.
- **The Federal Trade Commission.** Monitors complaints related to consumer credit issues. Contact the Consumer Response Center at 6th St. & Pennsylvania Ave., NW, Room 240, Washington, DC 20580 or call (202) 362-2222 (TDD/TTY: (202) 326-3502. The Web site address is `www.consumer.gov`.
- **The National Foundation for Consumer Credit.** Helps consumers establish a budget and repay creditors. For the office nearest you, call (800) 388-2777.

Appendix E
Addresses of federal agencies

The various federal consumer credit laws presented in this book are enforced by federal agencies. If you would like further information or have a particular credit problem that you would like addressed, you can contact the appropriate agencies.

- If your problem is with a retail department store, consumer finance company, all other creditors, and non-bank credit card issuers, credit bureaus, or debt collectors, write to:

  Division of Credit Practices
  Federal Trade Commission
  Washington, DC 20580

- If you have a problem with a particular national bank, write to:

  Office of the Comptroller of the Currency
  Deputy Comptroller for Customer and Community Programs
  Department of the Treasury, 6th F1.
  L'Enfant Plaza
  Washington, DC 20219

- If you have a problem with a particular state member bank, write to:

  Federal Reserve Board
  Division of Consumer and Community
  Affairs
  20th and C Streets, N.W.
  Washington, DC 20551

- If you have a problem with a particular nonmember insured bank, or if you are uncertain of your bank's chartering (state or national), write to:

  Federal Deposit Insurance Corporation
  Office of Consumer Compliance
  Programs
  550 17th St., N.W.
  Washington, DC 20429

- If you have a problem with a particular savings institution insured by the Federal Savings and Loan Insurance Corporation and a member of the Federal Home Loan Bank System, write to:

  Federal Home Loan Bank Board
  Department of Consumer and Civil Rights
  Office of Examination and Supervision
  Washington, DC 20522

- If you have a problem with a federal credit union write to:

  National Credit Union Administration
  Office of Consumer Affairs
  1776 G St., N.W.
  Washington, DC 20456

Many of these federal agencies have regional offices. Check your local telephone book under "United States Government" to see if there is a regional office near you.

Appendix F

Federal Trade Commission offices

The Federal Trade Commission is the agency responsible for enforcing the Consumer Protection Act. If a company has violated your rights under any of these laws, you can file a complaint with the nearest regional office.

Headquarters

Pennsylvania Ave. and Sixth St., N.W.
Washington, DC 20580

Regional offices

1718 Peachtree St., N.W.
Atlanta, GA 30367

10 Causeway St.
Boston, MA 02222

55 East Monroe St.
Chicago, IL 60603

8303 Elmbrook Dr.
Dallas, TX 75247

1405 Curtis St.
Denver, CO 80202

11000 Wilshire Blvd.
Los Angeles, CA 90024

26 Federal Plaza
New York, NY 10278

901 Market St.
San Francisco, CA 94103

915 Second Ave.
Seattle, WA 98174

Appendix G

Other books by Bob Hammond

Repair Your Own Credit, 2nd Edition, Career Press

Repair Your Own Credit is for anyone interested in the truth about credit repair. Learn the inside secrets used by credit repair companies to "erase" bad credit, create new credit files, and add years of positive credit history to your credit report. This book exposes the scams that have given the credit repair business a bad name and teaches you how to avoid getting ripped off by unscrupulous operators.

Life Without Debt, Career Press

This companion to *Life After Debt* provides advanced strategies for surviving in this credit-oriented society. It reveals inside information about the credit system, from credit cards to home financing, from student loans to co-signing for family members. It also contains special sections for dealing with the IRS, auto financing, bankruptcy, and the psychology of debt and spending. Learn to save thousands of dollars on mortgages, auto loans, and credit cards.

Credit Secrets: How to Erase Bad Credit, Paladin Press

Credit Secrets: How to Erase Bad Credit, Paladin Press

Credit Secrets contains a detailed description of the identification systems used by each of the major credit bureaus, along with dynamic strategies for circumventing the system and starting over with a new credit file. It also describes a unique method of "losing" your bankruptcy files and deleting any reference to filing for Chapter 7 or Chapter 13.

How to Beat the Credit Bureaus: The Insider's Guide to Consumer Credit, Paladin Press

In this intriguing follow-up to his best-selling first book, *Credit Secrets,* author Bob Hammond describes the deceptive web of information systems spun by the powerful corporate credit bureau syndicate and how it is used to victimize, humiliate, and defile countless innocent consumers. More importantly, it will show you how to take legal action against an unfair system—and win. Includes documented successful lawsuits against major credit-reporting agencies. This book is a must read for every American consumer.

Index

D

E

F

H

I

J

L

M

N

O

About the author

Bob Hammond is a nationally recognized writer, consultant, and consumer advocate. He is the author of *Credit Secrets: How to Beat the Credit Bureaus, Life After Debt, The Credit Repair Rip-Off,* and *Repair Your Own Credit.* A highly sought-after speaker, Hammond has been a guest on hundreds of radio and television talk shows throughout the country.

Hammond previously worked with Riverside County's (CA) Greater Avenues for Independence (GAIN) program, the country's most successful welfare-to-work program, and was instrumental in establishing the county's Alternative Dispute Resolution Program. He has also worked as an arbitrator for the Better Business Bureau, as an investigator for the Fair Housing Council, and as a consultant to Consumer Credit Counseling Services of the Inland Empire.

Hammond received his B.A. in psychology and sociology from the University of the State of New York, Regents College and studied screenwriting at the Hollywood Scriptwriting Institute.

Hammond is currently working on a techno-thriller novel about alternate identities.